the
SUMMER
BETWEEN

the
SUMMER
BETWEEN

a novel

ANDREW BINKS

NIGHTWOOD EDITIONS

Nightwood Editions
Box 1779
Gibsons, BC Canada V0N 1V0

The book has been produced on 100% post-consumer recycled, ancient-forest-free paper, processed chlorine-free and printed with vegetable-based dyes.

Design by Michelle Winegar

Nightwood Editions acknowledges financial support of its publishing program from the Canada Council for the Arts and the Book Publishing Industry Development Program (BPIDP), and from the British Columbia Arts Council.

 Canada Council Conseil des Arts
for the Arts du Canada

LIBRARY AND ARCHIVES CANADA CATALOGUING IN PUBLICATION

Binks, Andrew, 1958-
    The summer between : a novel / Andrew Binks.

ISBN 978-0-88971-232-4

    I. Title.

PS8603.I56 S94 2009   C813'.6   C2009-901309-6

Entreat me not to leave thee, or to return from following
after thee: for whither thou goest, I will go;
and where thou lodgest, I will lodge:
thy people shall be my people, and thy God my God:
where thou diest, will I die, and there will I be buried:
the Lord do so to me, and more also,
if aught but death part thee and me.

—*Book of Ruth,* Chapter 1: 16–17

ONE

No sound. No wind washing the trees, water splashing in the tub or lapping the shore of the river below. She filmed us with her old camera, before sound was invented. The projector rattles too, like it's broken, but never is. I bugged her once to get a new one.

"This works," she says, wheezing, jugs swaying, and her arm skin flapping as she winds it up. Her red curls toss around like a mad chicken.

And there I am, all bright on the screen in a yellow plastic bathtub, the kind for washing babies. Except for me, nothing else has changed. The house is still small in the woods, some of the trees are only stumps now. That's all. We still have the plastic bathtub. And there's a happy kid, white behinded, who steadies himself. Slowly turns. Gummy smile. He slaps his hands against his stomach. He waves towards the camera. He starts pissing. He is me.

"Dougaldo's pissing!" they all shout like they never seen a baby piss before. It gets a laugh every time Mom shows it. She never asks me if it's okay.

"You got a little worm," says Peter McIvor.

"That was twelve years ago," I say. "Same as yours anyway."

"Is not."

"Is."

"Frogs' cocks look like worms."

"I'm not a Frog."

"Your dad is, so you are, too. French fried Frog."

I pull off my sock and whip it at Peter McIvor's face. Jeff and Geoff sit Indian cross-legs behind me. "Who's the girl? That your twin sister?" says Jeff. Even Peter McIvor, who walks more like a girl than I do, laughs with them. I pretend to laugh, too. Can't wait for Dad to drive them back to the harbour.

"So you don't forget," she says after they are gone.

"Forget what? I only remember what I seen in the films. I don't remember being a baby or that peeing stuff."

"I like to remember."

"Well I only started remembering a few years ago."

"Don't talk nonsense." She sings when she talks.

She used to sing for real, according to Dad.

8

"Why not now?" I said once.

"They made fun of her."

"Her singing?"

"Her jugs."

"What?"

"She's a big girl."

"So?"

"So some people made fun."

"Why?"

"Jealous."

"Of Mom?"

"Uh huh."

"Not anymore?"

"What do you think?"

And I think Dad wishes she hadn't changed shape, and that I'd change the subject.

"Where? At the Klondike? With Diamond Lil?"

"No," he sputters out like I said something stupid. "Church halls—places with pianos."

"They made fun of her jugs in a church?"

"Just the women. Men..." But he stops when she comes into the room.

"That why we don't go to church?"

"*Ta langue!*" He only speaks French when he swears. Mom doesn't like any of us to speak French at home: "If Grandma Montmigny insisted, then so do I!" Grandma Montmigny didn't allow French either, but the majority ruled in that

9

house, says Dad. And as for TV, if it's important, like news, or *People in Conflict*, or anything with Robert Goulet, then it's in English.

"No one has a camera you have to wind up," I say to her next time she has it out. She has to frig with the projector, too. Twiddles her fingers around the ribbon to make it do what she wants.

"Anyway, they say I look like a girl in that movie, excepting I have a dink."

She stops. "Who said?"

"Them guys, after you showed it on my birthday."

"*Them guys* are just jealous. They don't have movies they can watch."

"Or moms making them watch movies."

"Between you and your father..." and she sighs again while she tries to get the ribbon in the little "Jesus Murphy" slot thing, curls tossing forward.

"Jean, do the screen, I'm almost ready," she says all giddy.

He unbuckles the legs, zips the screen to the ceiling, but it snaps him like he's a big mouse in a trap. "*Jesu Crees!*" he says every time he pinches his fingers, which is a lot. His face scowls whenever he does this, even before he starts. But normally he has a face like them dads on TV, each one good-looking, dark hair, pointy chin. Like Ricky Ricardo.

"Move over Miss Chubbles," I whisper.

"Mom!" she hollers.

"Tattle-tale… *Chubbles*."

"Mom!"

"She's hogging the couch."

"*Crees tabernac!*" says Dad at the screen.

"Not in front of them."

"They've heard it enough by now."

"That's for sure," Mom sings.

He swears again when he hauls the projector onto the coffee table. Mom? She sighs, pinching the film in like thread through a needle. Pulls in her lips. When it happens, finally, she sits back on her heels, claps.

"Show the last-summer one," I say.

"Last summer's not ready," Mom says.

"Tom isn't in last summer," Margaret says.

"So?"

"So you want to see *Tom*." She says it like it's a bad word.

"Do not."

"Do too."

"How do you know?"

Dad snaps his newspaper, holds it up, stomps a foot and we know he means for us to hush up. He usually sits between us, heavy hands on our shoulders. Not tonight.

So for yet another time we're looking at me as a baby, then Margaret coming home from the hospital when I'm four. There's no Tom, not in this movie. He'd be the only good part.

I cried once when I fell out of our tree onto a broke bottle. Tom crouched beside me, while I squeezed my hand. Tears onto blood. His hand was warm on my shoulder.

"If I ever catch you within a mile of that half-breed!" Mom yelped as she stomped down the steps, all curls and jugs, yanking me away.

Mostly he just watches when I skip with Margaret or Joycee. He's not like the others when they make fun of me at school. ("Go play with the girls!")

"Better 'n being last pick on anyone's team," I wish I said.

But Tom just lies back on his elbows, his sharp eyes under his bangs. He skips, too, if we make the rope go real fast. Mostly he and me take off on those girls, on little sister Margaret and neighbour Joycee.

I only see him in the summer, and spend all year thinking about him. Tom. Tomahawk. The "half-breed." My summer friend. Wish I knew him in this part of the movies.

"Those guys are right. I do look like a girl."

"Nonsense," Mom says.

"What lovely *daughters* you have—Miss Harris said that."

"That was a long time ago," Dad says.

"When did you see Miss Harris?" Mom asks, looking at Dad like it's more a question for him.

"A long time ago," he snaps back.

"How *long time ago*?" she asks him.

12

"When she was here last summer with the rest of the gang, that's all. Am I right Dougaldo?" Dad says.

"All I know is I hate the beauty parlour," I say.

"It's cheap!" she shouts at me or Dad. Not sure.

Anyways, I keep my own movies of Tom in my head.

Maybe my arms aren't as thick as his, like a boy's are supposed to be. Mom calls me Mr. Skin and Bones. He's a year older. Be thirteen now. Armpit hair coming in.

"Follow me," he always says, and I can almost keep up but he's up the hill like some kinda jackrabbit or something, with legs at least as long.

Too bad it's only in summer I see him. My insides twist. I'm not even hungry. I wish she would show last summer's movies.

"Stop banging your knees," Margaret says.

"I wasn't."

"I found your drawings again," Mom says. "I don't see why you can't put them up on the wall."

"Don't want them."

Most of the year I don't want to know the months not going by. I don't see the reason for winter and all the waiting for the snow and ice to melt. So I draw pictures of the beach and boats. And us. The pictures are never any good. I fold them away where no one can find them. Even so, it all makes it take even longer.

Something about it, about the heat and the butterflies and the tickles. Summer is still too far away, and all I can do is try to sit still in the classroom—cold white walls, hard floor, buzzing white lights—staring out the window. I can see the mountains on the other side of the river and can even see the river because the dead trees got no leaves to hide it. Not till spring. Snow swirls where the bus will be to take us home. Try not to dream about summer.

For now Miss Huta makes us line up on opposite sides of the room and spell out loud. She gives us words like W-O-N-D-E-R-F-U-L and S-O-M-E-T-H-I-N-G. Kids write up the answers to homework I never do. I pretend to be busy. I duck under my desk that's too small to hide me. Old gum and dried snot sticks to the underneath.

"Dougaldo, you can put up the second exercise." She sounds more like a mallard quacking in the reeds than a teacher.

I stand up and the wood chair clacks back onto the floor for the hundredth time. I walk up slow. Open my book, and paper falls everywhere on the floor. Behind me, those kids keep laughing through their stuffy snot noses. The chalk sticks to the sweat in my palms. All I do is grind one spot on the board to look like I'm writing. Chalk gets shorter and shorter.

"Dougaldo, we haven't got all day."

I don't even remember that we got homework, or from what day. "Forgot it at home."

"But you're holding the book."

"Yes Miss."

Everyone snickers.

She sighs a real long Mom kind of sigh. "Go back to your corner."

Maybe no one told me about it.

"Now everyone pay attention," she says. I look out the window: wind's come up. But all I see is me chasing Tomahawk up that hill, soles of his brown feet flashing white.

My stomach hurts like I have to go number two. "Miss, can I be excused? Can I be excused, Miss?" Them other guys— Jeff, Geoff and Peter—smile at me like I'm up to something when all's I want to do is sit on the pot and not be in school. If I do number two, so much the better.

She sees them smiling, says, "You'll stay right where you are."

"But Miss."

"Hold your tongue child," she says like some old-fashioned bag out of *Anne of Green Gables* that she's always reading to us. We say, "Green Goobers."

The skin on my arms. They're the same arms that'll be swimming in the river when the summer's here. The same skin that was there last year, my only souvenir of it.

At recess noodly Chester McBride is skulking around the edge of the woods, so we chase after him. Underneath the snow is water. We sink to our waists. Our boots fill with cold water. Branches snap.

"Four eyes!" We all shout at Chester.

15

"Goggle puss!"

He doesn't come back and we figure he'll come in all late and wet and get heck from the teacher.

After school there's a police car and Chester's dad is there too. School bus won't leave. Chester's dad and the police and us all head into the woods calling him. "Chester! Chester!" None of us can walk in straight lines for all the melting water.

We hear shouts from into the forest and start to run, but stop.

From way off we can see something swaying heavy from a tree, bigger than a squirrel's nest for sure, and Chester's dad is trying to jump into the air. Cops all lift him and then they fall down together including the swinging thing. It's Chester. The cop gets up off the ground. We get closer and his dad, holding Chester, is shaking like he has a bad cough.

"He's dead," says someone, and then a grown-up tells us to go back to the school. Margaret's on the bus, I don't say nothing. The ride home is quiet. I pretend I'm asleep. Chester was no one's friend. No one liked him. No one knew him. I go to bed early.

At school the principal tells us guys who saw what happened to Chester not to talk. Everyone does, no matter.

"Chester McBride is dead," Mom whispers to me when I get home, next night. She's all weepy, but she never even met him. She doesn't even know who he is. "Did you know about it?"

"Yep," I say.

"Why didn't you tell me?"

"I just didn't."

"So I'm the last to know. For Christ's sake I had to wait for your father to tell me. Nobody tells me anything around here."

"It's my fault."

"Not unless you tied him up there."

"We chased him."

"He took the rope yesterday morning. That's why his dad came looking for him. That's what I had to find out today—by *phone*. I can't believe I had to wait to find out."

She was the first to tell about the little retard girl who went through the ice and about Mr. Whiteside being chopped up in the river, so I guess she wanted to be first with this, too.

Going to bed early again makes no sense with all the ruckus. "Why'd you say it's your fault?" Margaret's got a little frown when she doesn't understand things. Had one ever since she was a baby.

"Made him go to heaven, that's all," I say.

"What's that like?"

"Joycee's mom says streets are paved with gold and everyone's rich."

"Is Chester there?" she says.

"Everyone, unless you're real bad. Chester wasn't bad."

"Maybe he'll see Mr. Whiteside and the girl who went through the ice."

Cold, wet school-bus rides. Looking out the window, like we're trapped in a refrigerator on wheels. Snow strings along the side of the bus. And in the road, miles of snow blows white across our path until we reach the bend and turn off the highway. The sky and the ground are one colour until May or June. The trees bring the dark in for the rest of the ride. Snow in the light's path makes it look like we're floating in Margaret's souvenir globe of the Parliament Buildings. Farmhouse lights at the end of long driveways make me wonder who's in there. What are they doing? What are they saying? And when we pass Tomahawk's dark place, I think about him spending winter in the city. For now his place is all boarded up till the first days of summer.

Bus leaves us at the top of the hill. Me and Margaret tumble all the way down the driveway. Dad can't even get the car up and down, so he parks it down the road a ways, where the plow piles all the snow. He plugs it in there with other cars.

At the bottom is our house, looking like brown gingerbread, and that too much icing will cave it in.

Mom's in the window, making dinner. No sounds. She doesn't know we see her and her eyes always down. She washes vegetables and wipes her forehead with the back of her hand.

"Don't drip. I've told yous to take off your things out there."

"But we'll freeze."

"I'm sick to death of mopping this floor!"

"Can't we at least…"

"At least take off your boots? At least shake the snow? At least be dry?"

The *naloneum* tiles are warm. The house is cozy. We lie on the thick carpet in front of the TV. Dad says inside our house is the French national colours. But I checked and the French flag is blue and white and our carpeting is orange shag and the walls are real-looking fake wood, painted green. Mom says it's a dog's breakfast. But it's not the colours of that either.

"What's for dinner?"

"Fancy Franks."

"Yippee!" we say together.

All the smells you get of dinner that has names like Oriental Surprise and Sole Survivor and Margaret's favourite, Birthday Party Casserole, and on Sunday sometimes roast beef. Sometimes a thawed pie, frozen from summer. It goes fast.

"Homework until dinner."

"Can we watch Lucy?" says Margaret.

"Thierry La Fronde," I say. He's the handsomest musketeer—dark hair, dark eyes—even if he is on the Frog channel. Kind of looks like Tomahawk.

"It's my turn for Lucy."

"If we only had one channel instead of two you'd still fight," says Mom.

"We aren't fighting because we're watching Thierry." Margaret starts to cry, which means I won't be getting Thierry and it's her turn anyway.

"I had a call from your teacher."

19

"Okay, I don't want to watch Thierry."

"She says you never do your homework."

"She can watch Lucy."

"She says you daydream."

"She's wrong about the homework. She never tells me what I'm supposed to do."

"Have you done your homework?"

"Almost."

"Almost?"

"I don't get it."

"Then your father can help you—if and when he gets home."

But he won't help so that's okay. I go to my room.

Margaret feels sorry for me, I can tell, so she switches Lucy to Thierry for me. I can hear him over the wall, telling his friends what they should do next.

I sit on my bed, stare at my books. Margaret gives up and turns off the TV. She knocks on my door. "Want to play?"

Mom tries to wreck our fun: "Don't go wandering off in the dark. I don't want to have to call the police." You can hear everything because none of the walls touch the roof.

We go back outside.

We made a bobsled run that goes all the way to the river.

"You have to roll them bigger," I tell Margaret. She shoves boulders into the corners.

"We'll fly off if they're bigger," she says.

"If they're bigger we'll stay on the track."

"You roll them then. You always get the fun part."

"Fun? If I don't pack and smooth just right we could kill ourselves."

"I hate you," Margaret says.

I get that pain in my stomach, doesn't go till we slide. Margaret drifts down 'cause she's still too little to go fast. Snow is getting too soft now anyway. Tom would go like a rocket on this. He's fearless. He swims in thunder and lightning.

"What happened on Thierry?" I say.

"He and the Injun made blood brothers."

"What?"

"Blood brothers. They cut their fingers…"

"Why didn't you tell me?"

"You were sulking," she says.

"What else did they do?"

"They had to feed each other, give gifts, something in the Bible, too."

"Then what?"

"Then they were blood brothers forever. I think they said Injuns do it all the time."

"Wow."

Back in the house, the TV is on loud so Mom can hear it above kitchen noises.

"You'll cripple yourselves one of these days, like that boy they just had on the news," she shouts.

"You've never even seen our slide."

"Don't be cheeky."

"Be good at least until your father's home."

Mom says she can hear the car coming up the hill, has radar in the back of her head. Unless it's summer, me and Margaret can't hear the car. But when the lights go by at the top of the driveway, then we know it's him. We get washed up. Dad'll have his drinks and sit in his chair with his paper and it really is *his* paper.

"Is it ours, too?" Margaret says.

"No."

"What do you mean about his paper?"

"He's the *ed'tor*."

"What's that?"

"He gets to tell everyone what to do."

"Why?"

"Because he's so handsome." Mom used to say that. Even with his glasses on he's handsome because of his black hair. We don't have that. She doesn't say that about him anymore. But I think he looks handsomest of the dads at Baird's Landing.

Now he comes in at the kitchen door. Dripping and snowy. "Hi."

"*Finally*," she says.

He used to kiss her on the cheek, and before that it used to be the mouth. He used to come home earlier, too. Not so now. Not since last summer. Not since *Miss Harris*, says Margaret, like Miss Harris was a time.

"Don't drip on the floor." (She used to say, "How was your day?") "Any time off this winter?"

"Not anymore, not the good old days."

"That's for certain," she says. "Holed up here all winter."

"We can't afford the city."

"What's a blood brother?" I say.

"A what? Don't interrupt," Dad says.

"Children should be seen and not heard," Mom says.

"Thierry and a guy made blood brothers."

Dad laughs. "Some Indian thing."

I look at Margaret and she looks like she can't hear them. Hands on her chubby chin or picks her nose and eats it while she pretends to watch the TV.

They used to be happy. I seen the car in our home movies, not the same one. "Big blue Buick," Dad says, all round on the corners and driving real slow down the driveway and you see mostly green leaves and sun and the dark blue car behind that until it parks. You can see Dad driving it, looking young and even handsomer, too. I don't remember that either. Just from the movies, like they were the only happy times.

After our Fancy Franks, Mom settles into cutting and pasting her films, and Dad behind his paper. I walk to Tom's cottage, no wind. The moon lights my way. Breath floats in little clouds around my head. When I get there, I peek through the boarded-up windows. In winter, it's still and quiet, dark all day and all night in there. I trudge circles around his house, in the snow, and punch my hands together over and over to keep

23

warm. I think of summer like I can see it all waiting under the snow.

I stand on the steps. The snow has drifted onto the screened-in porch, where they eat their meals. I spot his paddle, the one he uses for the canoe and boat and even to swat frogs. Almost new. Blue-greenish label—he calls *terk-oyz*—on the blade. I remember where his hand holds it mostly; it's soft and dull, the shine rubbed off. If I can get in, I can touch it. The door's never locked but now the snow keeps me from opening it, all piled against the other side, blown in on the floor. I shove a little and a little more. Pull off my mitt. Reach out. My bare fingers almost touch, thinking of his hand, soft and rough at the same time. Cold bites into my fingers. Touch it quick then put my mitt back on.

The moonlight reflection keeps me from seeing the old couch we sit on, further in, past the window, our feet touching, watching cartoons.

"Get outside," Tom's dad always says, like he's always in a bad mood.

In summer it's dark in, and bright out. Once you're out, you're out, too many noises to go back in: birds, water, kids, boats. But now the only sound is snow scrunching, and if I stop, then everything is quiet except for a breeze in the trees, maybe some branches clacking, and snow thudding into the ground. No, there's no TV in there now, just newspapers on the floor and some mousetraps. No comics or books or nothing.

I close my eyes and see us on the couch. My head is on Tom's lap. I never did that, but in my mind he pats my head like Mom used to. I walk a few more circles. My hands are cold now and the moon's gone behind the clouds. I rewalk my path and look back every few steps. Something Margaret said makes my heart thump. I walk faster, too. If Thierry made a blood brother with the Injun, maybe Tom and I could do that.

"Where on earth have you been?"

"Tom's place is okay."

"You're *not* to go wandering around there," Mom says. "It's dangerous, these places in the winter. Snow or ice could fall off the roof and we'd never find you till the thaw. And another thing, don't *ever* let me catch you near the river during breakup. Besides, if the ice doesn't get you, the ghost of that little girl will—those city folk wouldn't come here if they knew about it."

"Just watching out for break-ins—everything's fine."

"You're playing with Geoff this weekend."

"Do I have to?"

"His mom's driving him over."

"He's a whiner."

"We're having hot dogs and his mom's baking a cake."

"Alright."

Margaret's drawing a map with her crayons.

"What did they do?" I ask.

"Who?"

"Thierry and that guy."

25

"When?"

"The blood brother thing."

"They did things. Like I said he gave that Injun guy a gift, then they said something and had something to eat…"

"But what did they do with the blood thing?"

"They had to do all this stuff first, then they cut their fingers and mixed the blood together. It made me sick."

On the weekend Geoff brings his Titan rocket his dad bought him in town. Even though it has real gunpowder in the engines, it somersaults into the wet snow. It doesn't even go five feet.

"Gemini into the ditch!" I shout.

"Took me six months." He's mad.

"Any more engines?"

"They only give you enough for one try. They don't trust kids."

"Maybe it's a law. Do you think it's a law?"

"No!" he shouts. But he doesn't cry. Not like I can make Margaret cry. All's I have to do is tease her about being chubby.

"You're not fat," I say to her. "Just chubby."

"Mom, he called me *chubby*."

"Let's watch Lucy," I say, even when Thierry is on.

"But Thierry's on," says Margaret.

"I don't care, let's watch Lucy."

She won't let me be nice. I do something else, and she knows I'm just trying to be nice so she tries to find something

26

else to cry about. Anyway all I care about is I have to know more about blood brothers.

"You play fair!" shouts Mom, as if she knows what we're doing.

Until summer, grey all the time. "The Valley Effect," says Gutburn (no joke on teacher's name). "Clouds sit over the valley and stay for longer than they're supposed to." Something like that. We'll have a test. I'll fail.

He says the Indians took the white man up our river, the very same valley, too. "What's a blood brother?" I say, but he's onto the voyageurs now.

We scream after recess when our toes thaw and circulation comes back. It's not normal being bound up like those Egyptians, the mummies, with our faces frozen and our wet white skin shivering underneath like it had been in a hot bath, excepting for it's cold for way too long. Poor skin only seen the sun for maybe two months per year. Soon though, in the schoolyard, we are all making the best of the thaw. We crush through the tunnels in the snowbanks and dig rivers to drain the yard into the ditches.

The last day of school is the best; the first, the worst. Every day in between, I watch the hands of the clock, especially from recess to 3:40. It goes backwards if it moves at all. It's true. Forward only when it knows you're watching.

TWO

May. Three weeks, two days till the end. We find a page from a soggy nudie magazine left on the ground from before winter. Peter McIvor grabs it but I see a picture of a bare naked guy who is kneeling by this lady, dark hair in their privates, even the lady, same colour as the hair on her head. Peter's waving it at me. "Homo!" he says, and then waves it in my face and pulls it away. He can keep it.

"Dougaldo Montmigny hit me with an elastic. Teacher. Teacher!" says Jenny Westham.

I give up being good.

"Dougaldo, I am too busy to be your babysitter," teacher whines and everyone laughs. Geoff, Jeff and Peter, too.

Everyone has to tell on me.

The school, the classroom, the hallways are all louder in May. We slide the windows open. Curtains and blinds flap, doors slam loud like the wind blasts them shut. I can't do anything besides stare out the window, watching the poplars change in the woods with each breeze. Sometimes green, sometimes silver. Days go faster. I like giving back books I don't want to see ever again.

I play hooky on Sports Day. The men teachers roll their sleeves over their hairy white arms. The women's high heels sink in the ground. Hair blows in everyone's face as if the wind was something new.

"All's we did was sit against the wall," I say.

"Where?" Mom says.

"On the other side of the school. No one knew where we were."

"Exactly."

"But they didn't notice anyway, and we weren't far. Sports Day's just something to keep us busy."

"I don't know if summer is going to be better or worse with you at home."

"They just thought I was sick anyways."

"You told them you were sick?" says Mom. "If you lie about being sick you'll get sick."

"Just not feeling well. It's true. I had to lie down."

"Lie in the sun? Why didn't you tell the nurse?"

"She doesn't like me ever since I was looking for that Aspirin."

"I can't believe this."

"You were supposed to tell them I was sick, like you did before," I say.

"No dinner."

"But…"

"You can *but* to your father."

We giggle when Miss Huta (Hooter), kicks off her shoes, gets on her knees to write on the bottom of the blackboard.

"I like the stockings with the black lines up the back," I tell Peter.

"Why doesn't she wear them in winter?"

"Quick, look, she's in her piggies!"—we call them that.

At Peter's place, we get rough. "Want to tickle each other's feet?" and before I can answer, Peter tackles me and pulls at my shoes and socks until we're both tickling and kicking like mad.

Makes me want to pee. Like shinnying up a tree.

"You're a homo."

"*You're* a homo!" and then we kick and tickle even harder.

But Tomahawk's are more fun to touch. His feet and hands are like warm bark, like I think an old person's might be. I've only touched them by accident. He's not a homo. Thierry La Fronde isn't. And I bet if we were blood brothers, I'd be part Injun, too, and he'd be part me.

There goes my stomach.

He's there in our family movies, real little kid, the same only darker and sitting out back on a baby picnic bench and there we all are, eating hot dogs with ketchup and mustard (*mouse-turd*, we say), the sun shining down on my bangs making me and Margaret look like two little girls, again, and him even darker in the shade.

Another day before the end of school, Teacher tries to keep us busy by singing that song "Green Grow the Rushes O," three groups starting up one after the other. And when we get to the part about the lily-white-boys, we laugh and point. What's a lily-white-boy, anyway? Maybe me.

"Dougaldo Montmigny picked his nose and wiped it on my desk."

Jenny Westham can't take a joke.

"You farted." If I say something like that it'll seem like I had to wipe a booger on her desk to get even. And getting even isn't so bad. Even so, teacher sends me to the principal's office. No strap. Just sitting cross-legs in the hall. Injun style. My hands on my head. The music drifts out of the classrooms, down the hall, past the flapping blinds into the trees. Wind slams the doors and blows the winter far away. Little girls glare at me when they go to the toilet, then march back to their classes, noses in the air.

My desk is already in the corner of the class because of something I did before that I can't remember anymore. Teacher can't keep me anywhere but out in the hall, and that's way too far away, so she keeps me in the classroom and ignores me.

There's a class party, Freshie and chips and more being-nice stuff. Report card is lost in crusty paintings and glue collages and Popsicle sticks. I gather it up, with a hat, mitts, and stiff stuff all dusty out of the closet—most of it isn't mine. The end of school takes too long, but the best part is we don't have to stay for the whole afternoon. The bus has to take us home early. There are way more cars on the highway, too, stuffed with everything for summer: blankets, towels, groceries, clothes, kitchen stuff, books, even old televisions. You can't even see through the windows there's so much stuff and they all slow up the traffic.

"You can eat cattails," I say.

"Can't," Geoff says.

"Injuns did. I know that. They ate them like hot dogs." (I know that, 'cause of the Injun who told me, who I'm going to see after a whole year.)

"If they did then they died," says Geoff.

"Nope. Made pancakes out of them, too."

It's the only thing I know that he doesn't. He knows everything else. He can name practically every star, tree, flower and cloud. It's good he lives at the harbour, not Baird's Landing.

The Trans-Canada is crowded now and slow, past town and past the bakery. I know which building is the bakery with the smells so strong you can even smell them in the school bus, like when Mom tried baking her bread. The whole house smelled like a bed you been in too long, too cozy. Now she only buys it and keeps it in the freezer.

We keep going, past the Royal Burger. Sometimes with Mom and Dad we eat there if traffic's bad or we're bad. After that, houses are less, until just one here, one there and soon there's just countryside and farms.

The bus creeps along the Trans-Canada through places where cowboys and Indians and saloons were in the olden days. You can still see the words *Klondike Inn* painted on one place.

I see me and Tomahawk, the cowboy and the Indian, feathers and cowboy boots. Hold up our hands and say, *How.* Look in his dark eyes, his feet strong on the ground, steady legs. Our hands touch, too. My daydreams come closer and closer to me. Soon they'll just be what is.

"The real Klondike is farther," says Geoff.

I ignore him.

"Helium is actually safer for a balloon," he says. "More than hydrogen."

"Oh yeah?"

Even though he's smarter, he still ordered Sea-Monkeys out of the comics and when they grew you couldn't see them for the scum. He even ordered the ball to put them in and hang around his mom's neck for her birthday, but it got there broken in the package. Also, his Titan rocket was a dud.

"If you're so smart what does biblical mean?"

"From the Bible. Everyone knows that."

"I just wanted to make sure you know."

"Where'd you see it?"

"In the 'cyclopaedia, under blood brothers."

"Blood brothers?"

"My project."

"Means you have to look it up in the Bible I guess."

"We don't have one. Don't think we do."

"Everyone has a Bible."

Off the Trans-Canada, I can tell—even if my eyes are closed, the sound of the road's gravelly. Sometimes in the car we stop here at a burned-out bus called the Wayward Bus. It sells ice cream, fries. You wouldn't buy a burger there. Dad's sure people died from the burgers. He says they wrote about it in his paper. Says they use roadkill, like raccoons and skunks. That's usually when Mom hushes him. I been there with Tomahawk—his dad's a policeman and he took us.

"You have a blood brother?" I say to Geoff.

"I have a real brother. My mother says that's enough. She says enough is too much."

And maybe in Mom's movies I see more of us in front of the Wayward Bus. Margaret, little with her bangs cut high, me dancing around until I get a swat on the head, and then trying

34

to eat melting ice cream. Mom isn't in the film. There's only one time I remember her being in the picture.

After that, we drive past a signpost of names on arrows for strangers to find where people live, and then the bus speeds up with no one in front of us and we bomb through miles of birch and elm on a straight dirt road. If it's still light out, you can see the graveyard, mostly hidden by elderberry because it's swampy around there.

Then down a steep drop. Every driver (bus driver included) honks the horn. You'll feel your stomach in your throat and that's why we sit at the back. Even so, we feel our stomachs wrench and our bums lift off the seats.

"If we were sixteen feet above the ground and the bus shot us fast enough we'd never land," Geoff says.

"We'd land sometime. We'd have to."

"Nope. We'd keep falling because the curve of the earth would keep us from landing."

Well he's the genius, not me. I can see us sitting in the air going around and around looking at stuff all the while: the Eiffel Tower and China, too.

Then we come to the harbour, and Geoff's got to get off.

"Come over for swimming lessons," I say. He has to. Harbour's no good for swimming with its snapping turtles. It's good he's got his own friends anyway. I only like him for school. I got Tomahawk all summer.

35

Madeline's house means you're at Baird's Landing. Madeline's is a mile from our house and close enough even Mom can walk. Sometimes I seen a light on in Madeline's house or seen her walking from the store back to her house after locking up. I wave. She always waves even if she doesn't look our way—waves like she's waving you off, like you're a bothersome fly or something, like she wants you to get the heck away. I don't see her now.

"What does she do?" I asked Mom once.

"She runs the store."

"Yeah but she's not always there, and what about her sister?"

"It's her sister, that's all. Like you have a sister."

"What do they do?"

"When?"

"Like say when it's winter and them guys go away, where to?"

"To Florida, I've told yous that, and it's *those*, not *them*."

"How come we can't go? How come?"

"I've told yous what it's like. All guns, and shootings, finding people in chimneys and car trunks, ground up in meat pies and down wells…"

"We can take the monorail."

"But you can't," Mom says.

"I seen it on Disney."

"Not until you've gone practically all the way there."

"We can visit the *cousints*."

36

"It isn't safe—thieves and gangsters. Besides, your father won't take us."

I saw a picture of Mom's sister standing beside a car and she looks like a gangster. They like their cars, too—Americans. Maybe Mom's sister knows Madeline and her sister, because them guys go there every winter. Madeline and her sister are twins, only twins I've ever seen, they look a bit the same: wrinkly skin, red hair, deep voices and coughs that sound like Tomahawk's outboard sputtering on idle when we troll the river.

"What'll it be, kid?" (That's what they call me, "kid.")

"Licorice and Hires."

"And what for your kid sister?" That's what they call Margaret. It must be American 'cause how can my sister be other than a kid?

"Double Bubble."

"Don't do that licorice trick, kid. You use a straw from now on. Steps was sticky with cream soda and flies all last summer. Goddamn flies."

We turn a corner down to the river, the bus slows up, another stretch along the river, getting closer, closer. I catch a look into Tom's driveway before we shoot up the last steep hill but I'll have more time now to see his place, even though it's still boarded. Maybe tonight I'll go over and see if they came up early. Maybe he'll already be there and we can have a swim or

37

something. But then it's our driveway. And the bus stops so fast that the dust catches up to us. I'm out of the bus and down the hill. The house was painted a fresh coat of brown in the spring and you can barely see it for shade. Took the snow a long time to go, especially in the shadows, says Mom. Bus heads off down to the dead end, then it turns around and rockets back up the road. Fast, like Geoff's Titan should have.

"No doubt looking to kill one of you kids," Mom says every time the bus roars past.

"No more pencils, no more books..."

"Don't sing that," says Margaret.

"No more teacher's dirty looks..."

"Mom, he doesn't like school."

"You have sickness," I say. "Too-much-school sickness."

THREE

Early sun rises over the hills, up the river, through the house, warm on my face. I snuggle into bed but it's hot and I kick the covers on the floor. No more pencils, no more books.

I tiptoe across the living room. The sun sits straight ahead and shines red on the wall behind me. Funny how it'll get so much higher in another half a day.

Margaret left her sticky paper shapes on the floor so I lick and glue them all together. Now the little happy clown juggling at the circus is way more busy.

I spread today's funnies on the floor. Dad brought them from work last night.

Don't creak the door. Down to the river. Smooth like glass. Orange sun shoots across to me. Ripples follow Mr. Beaver to work. He comes all the way from where I can't see and goes past to just as far away.

Water's still high and cold from runoff. The dam up the river has to let through as much water as it can, at the beginning of the summer. Everything is under water, like where we'll put our beach towels and that, it's all still under water. I can't get out far enough to see Tom's place. Wet PJs make me want to pee, so I take everything off and throw it on a rock. Stand in my birthday suit. Piss in the river, too, to make ripples. Too early for Mrs. O'Brien and God to spy on me. The O'Briens got up to the Landing late last night, I heard their car. And as for God, he is off somewhere else where they need him. Everything's perfect here and he doesn't care I'm naked, that's how I was born. Everyone knows that except her, old lady O'Brien up there. Her with her bun smacked on the top of her head, like a circus clown. (I'd get a good swat for ever saying that.) Anyways, I wade into the river. I sit on some of the bigger rocks not under water. I pretend I never wear clothes. Sit down. Stand up. Put my PJs back on, and head up.

Margaret's up. She's seen what I done to her shapes.

"You never play with them," I say.

"I was making a circus." She's crying now.

"They're stupid. Can't make a person without their head shaped like a ball or a triangle."

"*M'énerve!*" shouts Dad, over the wall.

"Now I can't make my clowns."

"You woke them up," I say.

Dad's footsteps hit the floor. I put my *Children's Picture Atlas* down the back of my PJs just in time because he grabs me

40

by the shoulder and swats me where I put the book, without even checking if I did something wrong.

"*Jesu Cureestu!*" He drops me and holds up his hand just long enough for me to get away, while the atlas is pulling down my PJs. I race into my room and slide under the bunk.

Dad slams the bathroom door, more to wake up Mom than anything.

After that I'm thinking I'm not going to see if you-know-who is at the Landing yet. Maybe I should let him come to call on me this year. But it's not even breakfast yet. Maybe Tom and his folks got up to the Landing late, too. Maybe he's still asleep. I crawl out from under the bed and try being good for a while.

Soon Dad starts coffee and bacon.

"Jean, something's burning," Mom sings out, like he's stupid.

He sings back to her, "I know what I'm dooooo-ing."

He always makes the breakfast, and those are good smells, and sounds too—the bacon crackling and snapping with eggs on the same pan, and Mom still in bed or locked in the bathroom. "I hate this weather. I can't breathe, I can't move." Finally she waddles across the living room in her nightie, sheet wrinkle marks on her arms and dimples for elbows. I want to remind her how much she hated winter.

I eat mine and some of Margaret's bacon without her seeing. She won't eat it if I touch it or even pretend to.

41

"Can I have Snak Pak now?" She tries to sound like she's being good.

"Which one, honey?"

"You never call me honey," I say.

"You're not sweet," Mom says.

"Fruit Loops," Margaret says.

Only in summer she gets Fruit Loops. It made me barf the one time I had them and ate too many. The barf stung my nose, too, all morning long.

After breakfast, Dad and I get dressed. It's time to get the docks into the river and the rafts anchored in the deeper water while all the dads are here and maybe still happy about summer.

A footpath joins all the places. If you keep on it, you'll just keep going miles past Tomahawk's place and everyone else's too. Mom says it's made by them Injuns and Dad says by the loggers. I think it's Injuns because we still have trees, no one took them. Mostly evergreen. Evergreen is all that will live on the rocks, says Dad.

First we go next door to O'Briens' to get Mr. O'Brien and Joycee's big brothers. I stand behind Dad.

"Boy's growing up," says Mr. O'Brien.

From what I see Mr. O'Brien has grown, too—puffy middle with a shirt tucked over it all. Hair out of his nose and grey tufted on his head like grass.

"Like a weed," says Dad.

"Maybe this is the summer for Bible camp," says Mr. O'Brien. (They're all 'vangelis and do church stuff all year round.)

"Maybe even a job, eh Monsieur Dougaldo Montmigny?" Dad says.

"Joycee been asking after you," says Mr. O'Brien.

"I have not," she shouts from the kitchen screen door where you can't see in when it's light out.

"Too late Joycee," shouts her dad, and then there's no sounds. Grown-ups always shove kids together or yank us apart. Just can't leave well enough alone, as Mom says.

Dad knuckles my head. I pretend a smile.

Mr. O'Brien shouts for his sons Dan and Sam, who wander out still eating their PB and J, looking all gangly in no shirts, pimply pizza faces, hair like they just got up.

I follow behind the gang to Nate Goldstein's.

"How's the deli, Nate?" says Dad.

"Sheesh. I can't get far enough away. Busy, busy, busy." They stand close like old chums. "Marty's going to divorce me if I don't get a manager," he says, loud.

"Well I'm in the wrong business," says Dad.

"You are, as a matter of fact. You'll never make money at that paper. I don't understand it." Mr. Goldstein's handsome like Dad. Darker. Gold in between two teeth. His wife Marty, silver and black hair, on the steps painting her nails. Coffee and cigs.

"Got your gin there, Marty?" laughs Mr. O'Brien.

43

Marty doesn't smile. "No gin till noon. Coffee and cigarettes this morning Mr. O'Brien, can I offer you one?"

But Mr. O'Brien doesn't say anything. Like I heard, he doesn't "partake."

"Boy's growing like a weed. Needs a good haircut, looks like a tomboy," Mrs. Goldstein means me, even though she won't look my way.

"Heard about the McBride boy?" Mr. Goldstein says.

"Yep. Heard about the McBride boy," Dad says.

"Kids."

"Just never know."

Shake their heads and look at the ground. Chester wasn't an everyday kid in case they didn't know.

We keep going, getting more people. When adults have nothing to say, then every conversation's about me growing, or me having a girlfriend. And it's especially Mrs. Goldstein who thinks I'm practically a girl. I could talk about them like they do about me. I could tell "Whitey" Mr. White he's even sicker looking than last year, or tell Mr. McDonald I know a good dentist to straighten his piano teeth, and throw in a shoeshine for the top of his head, and old man Mapother that his hard beer belly looks like he's always ready to have a baby or a big poo.

And I don't know what religion the rest are but it doesn't matter because O'Briens' 'vangelis is your only way to heaven. And I know for sure they got a Bible if I need to find what the *Children's Encyclopaedia* says it said about blood brothers.

Each cottage and house is separated by trees but most of them are close enough you can shout to your neighbour. From Mapothers', you can see Tom's driveway and from the driveway, the rest of his place. I can't not smile. But I don't see him. His dad is Mr. Clark, the cop. He's there loading wood off the back of their station wagon, thick folds in the back of his neck. Wide back. Muscles bulge when he lifts, like Mr. Clean. "We always need him to do the grunt work," says Dad. But that's the kind of thing you don't tell another person to their face.

"Where's Cap'n Clark?" Dad calls to Tom's dad. Calls Tom "Cap'n Clark" because Dad says he's always out on the water.

"Tom's with his mom," he says. "She's sick." How do you help a sick mom?

"Martine not well?"

"Not sure, yet."

None of the men say anything.

His mom's tall, long black hair. Perfect almond eyes that Mom says all women want. A real Injun. They said he shouldn't have married her. They said it was a waste and those women always steal our men. Anyway she keeps mostly to herself.

Minus Tom, those are the main ones. We help anyone old or too busy, like Doctor Smiley or anyone, and sometimes we'll just go ahead and put in their raft or dock, and even boats down from the marina on the trailers.

By noon there's the gang of us travelling up the shore, back towards our place, dogs and everyone, some kids getting in the way. Most of the stuff is too heavy, even for a few strong men. And it's hard to get around the trees. Ice and high water has pushed everything up higher. Sometimes we have to flip things down the hill. Dogs and kids scuttle each time someone shouts, before a section of dock or raft flips.

And all through it they keep saying stuff like, "Good to see you're up again early George," or "How's the wife and kids?" in low grown-up voices while slapping their hands together.

"Where's Tom?" say some.

"Martine's not well," grunts Tom's dad as his arm muscles bulge and he pushes another piece up and over. Men raise their eyebrows when they see how strong he is. Others just stand and squint. Sky so blue and the water still as the air, until about noon-time when little breezes rush across and break it up.

"It'd turn their undies to ice if they knew what this place looked like in the dead of winter," Mom says more than once a summer. "White as the grave."

But Tom would know, if he didn't have to take care of his mom. Him and me could live here. In a log cabin. Two swallows through the woods, fishers over the water, not a sound. Hunt for dinner—fish, squirrels. Kill a lynx. Read comics. Eat our food. Wind blowing outside. Play cards. Take turns tucking each other in.

First thing I have to do is give Tom something for the blood brother ceremony. That's what Thierry did.

46

"Dougaldo, wake up!" shouts Dad, and I jump. "Quit dreaming of Joycee."

And the men laugh.

Boat bottoms squeal along the rock, down to river's edge, before they skid across the surface. The men float the rafts onto the water and drop their anchors: things like bricks, car engines and old washing machines. Mud blooms up from down under. But one of the rafts stands on stilts on the bottom of the river, a "*nomaly* of science," says Dad.

All of the men are pale or plain white, not real Landing folk, says Dad. Some skinny. Some with beer bellies. White shoulders, arms, noses, cheeks turning shiny red. Even though they rolled their pants they're all wet at the bottom. Some are soaked from tumbling in. And me, I'm everything—wet and burnt too. I guess if Dad could, he'd move us to the city and then we wouldn't be Landing folk either.

Joycee O'Brien's two older brothers don't look like the dads. Just as tall but backs pimply like their faces, and stomachs like they're always hungry. They reach for a log or a boat, and under their skin you can see the strands slide like straw, all ribs and ropey muscle, in floppy shorts, not wiry like Jimmy the swim instructor. No, not like Jimmy in his Speedo.

Dad and me run up the hill to our place for *refraîchissement*, as Dad calls them, and no one else would understand that.

Meanwhile, Mom is putting the last of the screens on. She wipes over the screen turning the spiderweb and dust into

47

white strings. She squeals when she finds animal poop or a dead mouse that didn't make it through the winter.

"Just getting liquid refreshment," says Dad.

"Well save one for me," she huffs with all the work.

Today they talk like they did until last summer, as if they like each other. Maybe they're just used to each other now, like me and Margaret.

I plug down the hill with some beers, over the same path the bobsled run took in the winter. All of a sudden, halfway down, I can sense something, and I remember Joycee's probably watching me from her place. I can't see her, but I know she's watching. She's prob'ly looking for Tom.

Now the men are tipping their heads back and draining the bottles. Some faster. Someone hands me a root beer. Mr. O'Brien and his sons won't take any of anything, they say. Mom calls them teetotallers. Other men tease and say beer is God's gift, and then try not to belch. After the beers, some men go, others come along and we keep moving down towards Big Red's (her brother, swim instructor Jimmy calls her that—I think she's more a "Fat Patty"). Jimmy's off in his speedboat with his friends from the harbour, and Big Red isn't around anyway.

Finally we get to the end of Baird's Landing—if you go along the shore there's nothing for about a mile except one abandoned cabin, no road up above—and the end of our work, too. Everyone heads back to their places. They all joke about sharing another beer. Adults always do that. And now the Landing looks more like I'm used to. Docks, boats, people. Soon the water will be lower. We can start to spy, too: look in windows in the dark, crawl under verandahs, hide in pumphouses.

"Can I go call on Tom?" I say. This will be a fight because it's too late in the day, so I flick a fly off Margaret's head and get a swat from Dad. I know it's time to keep my peace.

"He's with his mom," Dad says.

"Maybe she's better now," I say.

"Doesn't sound like it."

"Martine's sick?" Mom says.

"Sounds bad," Dad says. Grown-ups must have talked when I wasn't paying attention. Didn't sound bad to me.

"You kids stay away from there. I don't want you catching anything," Mom says.

"I don't think they can catch it," Dad says.

"They live like savages down at that end. Dougaldo, you should be playing with your sister. Geoff, too. He's a good influence. Sweet Jesus that boy is bright."

"Looks like cancer," Dad says.

"What's cancer?" Margaret says.

"Eats you up," Dad says.

"Jean!" Mom says. "It can make you sick, that's all."

Mom likes to be the one hearing and telling about dead people.

"It can kill you," he says back.

"We're not at the newspaper!" Mom says.

"Tom's mom's going to die?" Margaret says.

"You don't know that!"

We settle in with hamburgers and chips Mom made. Chips are the frozen kind that go in the oven. If Dad makes them he does it the French way, he says, and boils them twice in the oil. "You'll burn the place down," Mom says and "I can't get the smell out for days." It's true. But it's a good smell.

My stomach doesn't feel like any kind of food. I'll go see Tom tomorrow. I need to figure out what I can give him to start the blood brothers ceremony.

Dark comes late. Sounds that come with the dark too— through the screens now. Raccoons on twigs down to the river. A lonely whippoorwill, or a loon, out on the water. We're nestled into the chair and couch, me with the funnies I never got to read this morning. We don't have bedtimes tonight. Summer's the only time for no bedtimes says Mom. I can barely see Margaret under Mom's big arm, reading a story. I lean my back into Dad. The funnies swim away.

FOUR

Sun shoots hot through the trees. My bed's wet. "I wet the bed. Forgot my pill."

"Be good today. Your mom is whiny," whispers Dad.

"I am not!" she shouts. "You know where the clean sheets are. Going to be hotter than yesterday, they say. Change the bed before it starts to stink." Mom fans herself and flops into chairs, 'specially in front of Dad.

"When are you going back?" she says.

"Two weeks, that's it," Dad says.

"What am I supposed to do?" She frowns her shiny face. "Stranded."

"I have to go back."

It's his dream to make his newspaper "work." I heard his secretary Miss Harris say that last summer when she was here. He already had some good years, she said.

51

"Loneliness more than heat," Mom says.

"When the paper gets going we'll move into the city," he says.

"Is that *all* that keeps you busy?" she says.

"What's that supposed to mean?" he says.

"You know exactly."

"It's the paper keeps me busy."

He doesn't sound like he means it. And she hates it, except when he's here—then she hates him.

Someone else is holding the camera now. Mom thinner, still big jugs and curly red hair and with one of them long swirly dresses on that women don't wear now. Pretty, too. She's even smiling. I can't walk yet and there I am bouncing on her knee like an uncooked turkey and she and Dad happy like I never saw before. Dad is even proud looking. That's the one time I saw her in a film.

"It's that secretary," Mom says.

"*That secretary* has nothing to do with this," Dad says.

"Oh yes she does."

"You're imagining things."

"And so are you."

I stop listening. I'm still free so I go, besides I heard it. I know what they're going to say. Even when he takes time off from the paper, he doesn't really. He goes into town to check on things, he says. And she gets mad.

"They won't work if I'm not there," he says.

The day gets hotter and hotter.

Down at the beach, Mom ties a rope to a rock and floats on our paddleboard around the reeds. Tomahawk said she's like a beached whale, said he heard the other women say it. I never saw a beached whale. She says it's too hot up at the house and it must be true 'cause all's she likes to do is sit and glue together films and put photos of us in her books. Doesn't take pictures anymore. Maybe we aren't cute now. But she can't do that today in the heat, so she just lies there on the water. Face down in movie mags. Too bad I don't know if she's asleep for sure.

"Leave her alone," she says when Margaret starts to whine, so I guess she's awake.

"But…"

"Leave your sister alone."

"She…"

"Not a word. Go and get some water."

"But…"

"Now!" she says from under her magazine.

I take off up the hill before Margaret can follow me and ask where I'm going. I grab the empty buckets to get water from the O'Briens' well. Unlike a wishing well in storybooks, it has a tap. I check to see no one's out on O'Briens' step and that Joycee's brothers are nowhere near. You can barely see Joycee's place once the leaves are on the trees, even though it's next door.

53

I don't see Joycee. Joycee's mom and my mom are always pestering me to play with the girls.

"You're wild animals," said Mom once, and I know those are really Mrs. O'Brien's words.

I have to take off on Margaret, or both of them, even though they squeal on me. Joycee is from the city and one year older, like Tomahawk. 'Vangelis. I call her a city slicker and that gets her hot mad especially in front of Tom. Joycee's screen door slams a lot, too, but I know she won't come to call. She's too proud. Her mother doesn't like that, either. Me neither for that fact—girls calling on boys. But her mom says girls should not go to the movies, not even a drive-in, with anybody—even grown-ups. They don't have much fun, unless playing snakes-and-ladders every night is fun. I can feel her eyes now looking into my back. I know for certain someone is behind the screen. No wonder I always feel like I'm being watched at O'Briens'.

"Joycee, you're husband is here."

"No, just her boyfriend," and it's her brothers' voices I hear cracking from behind the screen door.

"More like her girlfriend!"

They make fun of me whenever they see me, which I try to make not too much.

The floor squeaks and I know she's come to shut them up and now they're all watching through the screen just because it's so good for spying when the sun shines on it. Finally Joycee opens the porch door and stands stubborn. Stubborn toes.

Stubborn hairy legs. Stubborn black curls. White face like an unbaked pie. Mom says she's a classic Irish beauty whenever we're around Joycee's mom, but to be honest she just reminds me of an ugly boy. Can't see her being anyone's girlfriend.

"You can't have our water," she says.

"Says *you*," I say.

She always starts with a "you can't," and then adds something like "our dock," "our boat," her "fishing rod," her what-have-you.

"Get lost," one brother says from inside.

"Lovers' quarrel," the other says.

"Joycee is in lo-ove," they start.

I wait until the buckets are full. They can't stop me using their water.

"Seen Tom?" she says.

"Maybe. Maybe not."

"Well I don't care."

"Me either."

"Don't you want to see him?" she says.

"Maybe. Maybe not."

"We can go together. I'm good as any boy."

"But you're not a boy."

She comes at me with her fists way back. I hide my head. She beats me hard.

"I'm better'n any boy, lookid you."

"It's look it, not lookid."

55

She keeps screaming, "Ha, you're like a girl, afraid of everything. You're not even good as a girl. Less, 'cause you can't even run in bare feet or shinny a tree."

"You'll never be a boy," I sing at her as I duck and run away.

Blue colours in our home movies make even hot days look cold, and there's this one of me and Joycee sitting naked on a rock surrounded by water, just hers and my backs, her arm around me, and we're looking out to across the river. Only maybe two or three years old. Like two girls.

"Hi Joycee." And now Margaret's here. Sings her words like Mom. Too bad she's not more of a worry to Mom because now we're supposed to play with her.

"We got to make tests for her if she wants to be in the club," says Joycee about Margaret.

"She did the tests last summer," I say.

"There's another test that she has to do to be a member of the club." As if making her eat toothpaste, saw a dead snake in half or shinny till her hands bled last summer wasn't enough. And I got heck.

"She did enough tests." I know I'll get real heck 'cause of Mom's mood with Dad this year.

Even so, we take off.

"I'm telling!" Margaret calls.

Joycee's taken fags from her brothers. Even if she's 'vangelis, she steals, and they smoke. Her brothers are almost old enough to get them from Madeline's or maybe farther away so no one'll tell. We go off in the woods. I put a whole bunch in my mouth just to get it over fast. Can't help choking, though.

"Let's go see Tom," she says, friendly all of a sudden.

"Nah, not now. Have to go."

And when she's back in her house, putting toothpaste on her tongue, I put the empty water jugs back on our step for later, and take off to see Tom.

The closer I am to Tom's place, the slower I walk. I try to look like it's not his place I'm headed towards. I try to look at other stuff than the direction I'm going. I look at things like the bees bouncing through the ditch grass. Wonder if Geoff's theory about the road shivering in the heat, and looking like water far off, is true. It looks like water just before the part where the road drops, and there just past the hill I see Tom's dark hair shining. Bangs cover his face.

He's crouched on the step. He doesn't see me.

Funny. Him just there, not knowing. Bobbing some pebbles into the walk, elbow bouncing on his knee. I keep walking slow-like down the hill, like maybe I'm not even going to his place. My throat narrows with butterflies up from my stomach. I can hear the gravel under my feet, or my breath? I need to give him something for the blood brother ceremony. Margaret says Thierry did that.

"Hi," I say.

He doesn't talk.

"Mom's sick?"

He gets up, walks towards the steps that lead down to the river. I follow him. He looks better'n last year. Hair growing out his armpits. Muscles. I can tell he had a haircut 'cause it looks like straw or hay sharp at the ends it's so even and straight. He goes down the steps and onto the dock. I follow him. His feet spread wide like thick beef each time he takes a step.

He stops, I knock into him and we're even closer when we sit down. We swing our feet over the water. No talk. I look at his feet. They're rougher than mine. Missing some toenail on his left big toe, but it doesn't look ugly—not like a dad's toe or anything. Still looks tanned all the way from last summer. He doesn't know I'm looking. He did stuff last summer like stick them in my face, and then I pretended it was gross when really I liked it.

Swung him on the hammock two summers ago, by his big feet, swung him higher and higher and he grinned till the rope broke and he cracked his head on the stump, only time I seen tears in his eyes. Mom rushed out. She thought it was me at first, and ran over to him, tried to hold him like she tries to hold me, but he just took off.

"You'll not be playing with that half-breed," she said. That's what she and Mrs. O'Brien call him. "It could have been you."

"His name is Tom, 'cause he's Tomahawk."

"I don't want that half-breed coming around here, he's nothing but trouble," she said. Since that time, either she hides in the kitchen or he waits for me behind the screen door, like a shadow. Both keep their distance. I get the dirty looks, too, if she knows he's there, like she gives Dad when he's home late.

"Are you half-breed?" I asked him. "Mrs. O'Brien says you are. What is a half-breed anyway?" He didn't say nothing. Maybe I talk too much.

Last summer, the phone was out after a storm so we headed up to Madeline's, hoping her payphone wasn't down, to tell Dad to bring hot dinner. The road was steaming and the rain had stopped, only dripping big drops off the trees, Mom was wheezing before we even got halfway. From the road we could see Tomahawk's mom was there, too. Her black hair hiding her face, like Tom's does, and what my mom calls her *almond* eyes. She was smoking. Mom stopped for a second, like she didn't want to go in, but I pushed open the door. Mom didn't look or say nothing. No hello. Just walked to the phone. Tom's mom just kept her back to us.

Mom faced the wall, finger in her ear. Everyone's back was to everyone and it was all quiet till Mom talked, but she practically whispered.

"When will you be home?" she said to Dad on the phone. "Power's off—so maybe bring something out from Royal Burg?"

Me and Margaret smiled like fools, like there was something we agreed on.

She hung up and turned to us. "It's just starting to rain there so they'll be getting the worst of it soon," she said loud to the whole, almost empty, place.

No one said anything—not Madeline or her sister or Tom's mom.

We walked past her again, no words. Back outside, me and Margaret squirming our hands from Mom's grip.

"You can tell by the way she looks," whispered Mom as if it was a secret or something bad (maybe it is), but his mom's like a picture and Tom's the handsomest guy I ever saw. Straight, shiny hair covers his ears. Eyes always narrow like he's thinking and nose like the beak of a big eagle I seen in the books.

"They live the same as we do," I say. It's not true. He knows things I don't—how to bait a good hook, where to find salamanders—and he's not afraid of the black water. He never talks much, just nods or grunts and so I fill in the spaces. Even when we pick raspberries along the tracks, if I'm quiet, it's only 'cause I'm eating. Anyway, Mom huffed and started wheezing and we had to slow up for her to get home in one piece.

"Well one thing's for sure," she says. "She got her trophy."

"What do you mean?"

"Never mind."

But today Tom and me just sit on the dock, close, shoulders almost touching. Finally his soft foot pushes mine, touches mine. He does it again, making it make ripples on the water, when it bounces out and back. It's my first time ever in the summer that I don't know what to say.

"Hateful monsters," says Mom when she hears that Joycee and me took off on Margaret.

"I was gettin' water."

"There's that wild lynx on the loose."

"On the French side."

"Ha, just like your father," she kind of chirps it out, or more like a squeaky door—quick and loud.

FIVE

"Swim lessons start today!" Mom sings. She fans herself with the yellow swim-lesson flyer someone slid under the door.

"There goes a day of fun," I say to Margaret. Stops you from an early start at anything 'cause for a half-hour swim instructor Jimmy shouts at you to *move, move, move*!

On the way down to the river I hear the tugboat, the first one of the summer. You can't see it yet, even if you can hear it. Not for a long time to come. I know Tomahawk will be wanting to go out to check up on it. Maybe we'll go after our swimming lessons. He's got to go to swimming, too, same as us.

Me, Margaret and Joycee hop along the flat boulders. It's all part of a big ledge, like a giant bear claw, up along this part of the shore. But the moms take the road this morning. They say they come to watch, but they just like to sit and gossip.

Swim instructor Jimmy's speedboat is anchored in the deeper water out from the ledge, nose high, with a Mercury 115 on the back. It looks like a rocket. It's the only racing boat on this part of the river and does it make a noise. Motor looks too big, just sitting there, but slick when it gets going with the rooster tail. Up here Jimmy is on his own as much as he wants and he has his own gang, too, mostly from the bay. Not like him though—they sleep all day, and then they drink and drive around in the river at night and go to the French side to drink more. You can hear it when they drop in at Jimmy's.

He walks along the dock like always, smooth skin and his Speedo. Even from here you can tell most of his body is muscles. He has red hair like his sister Big Red and up close he's covered with freckles. Even on his chest.

"Move it!" He says. And every time he shouts everything on him gets more muscley. Like the guys in the back of the comic books, where the big guy kicks sand in someone's face. Today he's yelling at kids even when they just tread water.

Everyone's there. All the moms. They like Jimmy, too. Swimming lessons are at Tom's because the water gets deep quick and Tom's dad built a good sturdy dock. And you can jump off the dock or dive. Not like our place.

Tomahawk bobs in the water. Duck-dives away. Bottoms of his feet flash and he's gone. Big Red is there on shore. Fat with her red hair. Patty's her real name. Fat Patty.

Lessons started out easy as trying to count Jimmy's fingers under water, but now it's scary trying to survive while Jimmy gets us to drown each other.

"In the water!" he screams, his body tight. "First one drowns the last!" This time we get a warning.

After that, we all have to tread water and hope no one is going to sneak up and surprise-drown us. But I keep looking at Jimmy's big feet even bigger than Tom's and the lump in his bathing suit and even so I know if I don't pay attention I'll get dunked. But today he's wearing the black Speedo with a yellow stripe on each side and his privates shoved in, and from the side you can see the shape, like a big hooked nose. Someday I want a Speedo—if it makes me look strong and grown up like Jimmy.

All I can think about is what his looks like. Like I saw in that magazine picture at school—the man who was kneeling and his rat looked like a big mushroom or a giant ripe strawberry. The other part of it looked like the hose into the pumphouse. The more I think it's dirty the more it sticks in my head. What colour is his? Is there red hair around it? Must be, because hair runs from his belly button down, so it must. Freckles? Do they stretch when he gets a boner? Does he get boners? Has he ever touched it? He must have to touch it to tuck it in his Speedo. If Joycee's brothers look like that you can't tell. They don't hang out with Jimmy. They do more churchy kind of stuff even if they're bad sometimes. I wonder if...

Fingers stab hard on my head. Squash me down to everything dark. No air. No sound. Weed tops. Rising muck. Kick, scratch and punch and punch and kick to the yellow. I jerk back and forward but there's no way up. It's other feet I'm under until finally I pull myself to the darkness out and away and then up, up, up. Suck in all the air. Throw my arms every way. How long was I under? All of them laugh and look around like "What happened?" and "Who's next?" I'm thinking Jimmy got Tom to do it. He probably saw me staring. I paddle up close to where Tom is treading and no one can make me be anywhere else. All's I know is the dark water scares me but won't keep me out. Besides Tom can save me even if he's the one that tried to drown me.

I dreamed Tom pulled me from the water. He carried me up on shore. Maybe it was too late and he cried and carried me to the bunkhouse or maybe it wasn't too late and he tried to save me and put his lips on my mouth—I knew he'd save me. I even relaxed my legs and my body in that dream because the worst that could happen was that I'd pee the bed.

But my dream of me dying is not like the gory stories Mom whispers to the other ladies at swim lessons. They don't bother me as much as they excite me. I've heard them all. Even from the water I can tell she's onto her favourite story. "He fell out," she's saying, spreading her hands like she does after she puts on nail polish. "And while his life jacket kept him floating the boat circled over him again and again, cutting him up into smaller and smaller pieces, like pieces of *stewing beef*!" Always the same, arm circling now. She looks like she's telling them how to ice a cake.

"Even a life jacket isn't failsafe." All the women nod in agreement, even though they've heard this story so many times.

It was different when Dad told it to me.

"We were standing by the car trying to help him into the back."

"So he wasn't stewing beef?"

"Just bleeding, mostly from one place."

"Was he all one piece, then?" I say.

"And all of a sudden I'm shoved in the back of the car too and we're on our way to the hospital," Dad says.

"Bleeding on you?"

"On everything and then his body just got soft and heavy and that was it and don't tell your mother I told you."

There's always something I'm not supposed to tell her. Like if I'm in town with Dad. We stop somewhere. I sit in the car for a long time, or read comics at the drugstore.

"Just tell your mom we were at my work, don't want to spoil her surprise," he says.

I never would. Besides I do stuff I don't want her to know about.

66

But Mom tells the stories as if she saw them. "And then there's the little girl who walked out onto the ice one winter…"

She doesn't move at all, for this one. It's a true story. I even seen her on the school bus. A slow learner with wavy dark hair, never brushed. Coat never buttoned. Real red lips like a doll's, and white skin. Idiot mitts but she never wore them. Kind of short like she didn't grow when she was supposed to.

"…and they never found her body." After that no one lives in her house anymore. They still don't, but we can't go there— not like we do the other abandoned ones.

"It's not the end of the story," says Mom. "Her ghost walks there, an unsettled spirit—maybe someone who loved her killed her." And then Mom is quiet like she gets before she's going to cry, but I think she's just pretending.

She hasn't talked about Chester yet. Maybe it scares her he killed himself. Maybe she's still mad I didn't tell her. Maybe she doesn't want to use up all her stories.

I hear it all in my head even though she's over there, on the shore, and I'm treading here, black water under me…

"Duck dives—now!" hollers Jimmy. "And don't come up for fifteen feet, or fifteen minutes!"

Balloon cheeks of air push at my lungs. Got to stay close to the top. See through the yellow, far enough under to be out of sight, and make Jimmy think I'm trying. I don't want to be the one to find the body of the retard girl. Boulders shove up from the bottom. One so big it has to be marked, you can see it clear from any boat, but most boats hit it and it makes Dad laugh.

It sits just under, waiting. If the water's low like in August, or they don't let much through up at the dam for a spell of hot weather, you can see the top of it sticking out of the water.

Joycee the show off, plopping black curls and pie face, first off the end of the dock, smack into the water. I cannonball, but open up like a scared chicken before I hit. Joycee's black slit eyebrows are always raised like she thinks you just did something stupid. She knows so long as I'm afraid, she can boss me around.

"Pool's way deeper at school," I say.

"But you can see the bottom," she says.

"Not if I close my eyes."

"No one swims that way."

Once, last year, I forgot my swimsuit. I told Hub, the school gym teacher. "Go in your birthday suit," he said, friendly like, not mad or anything.

I swam the whole class naked. I didn't mind. Wasn't a punishment, he just didn't want me to miss swimming. Me either. And that day there's older ones in the shower and we see one guy and say he's got a banana hanging down from him and he just kept standing there letting the water run off it like he was taking the world's longest pee. I wonder if mine'll look that way when I'm grown up. Bananas, strawberries, mushrooms? What was God thinking?

We pop back to the surface. Me first like always and Jimmy yelling at me to go back down as one by one heads come up for gasps.

Other than trying to drown each other, we have to do artificial respiration. Last summer I had to put my mouth on Joycee's and barfed my breakfast into the river. It floated and no one swished it away. They all laughed until I didn't care. I made them laugh.

Everybody pairs up today. Joycee stuck with Big Red 'cause Big Red grabbed her arm. I grab Tom's arm (Joycee won't look at me now). I lie on my back, close my eyes. Tom's soft lips open over my mouth. But it's not like lips. I thought of his feet at school in winter every time I had my hand on my face, and I pretended it was his foot, and now I don't have to pretend his lips are on my face, and lie there and let his hot air fill my cheeks, and then my belly, up and down, the wind inside of me. No one knows what I'm thinking. If I really was dead, the warmth of his air would make me alive. As a matter of fact, I would pretend to be dead for a while longer.

"Off the dock, time's up," yells Jimmy. "Off before I drown each and every one of you." And I'm dizzy. I don't get a chance to save Tom, not this time. No time to switch partners. I'll never get used to being drowned. Tom doesn't talk to me, just does as he's supposed to, like always. Mom said he's like that because his father's a *tyrant*. Don't ask if that's in the dictionary.

On the shore I look at Tomahawk and wonder what his thing is like now he's getting older. Prob'ly hairy.

I follow him. "Tomahawk," I say, quiet, so Joycee doesn't hear, and I can call him that, *Tomahawk*. He just keeps going.

69

Not a word. I don't want to say it again. I think his mom must be real sick. He'd go out to see the tug any other day, I'm sure of it. He didn't even say a word to Joycee. And she won't talk to me.

To get onto the road we have to walk up the hill and past Tom's. Joycee and Margaret have run ahead but Mom and Mrs. O'Brien (balancing that bun on her head) lean into the hill like it's Mount Everest they're climbing, tipping back and forth with each step, hands on their knees pushing to get up there. They say stuff about getting old and the hill getting steeper every year.

"You kids watch out for cars!" shouts Mom to anyone listening. "You'll be the death of me."

I'm glad they're going slow, so I can stay behind them and get a peek at Tom, or let him see me just walking along like I have no plans, no friends.

"They say he's trying to kill her," says Mrs. O'Brien. "Him and that nurse are in on it, keeping her all drugged up like that."

I shut up. Like Mom says, children should be seen and not heard. They're still talking about Tom's dad.

"He's been sneaking off to see Doctor Smiley's wife for years," says Mrs. O'Brien.

"And she's her nurse?" says Mom.

"The *very* nurse," says Mrs. O'Brien. And I think Mom's jealous she didn't get to tell Mrs. O'Brien something she didn't already know.

"Well it makes sense then," says Mom. "What a waste, if you know what I mean."

"Lord help that godless woman," says Mrs. O'Brien.

"Amen," says Mom, like she means it.

I race ahead to find the girls.

Back at our own beach, Joycee and Margaret beat me onto the paddleboard, scraping the bottom on the rocks. It can hold three kids most of the time, or one of my mom—never room for sister Margaret except today.

"You won't get far before lunch!" I shout.

They float around the reeds in the shallow water hanging their arms over the side and turning stones, saying stuff I can't hear, probably looking for crayfish, frogs too—bait for Joycee's dad, or Margaret catching minnows, her little fingers flicking them from the net into a jar.

"You have to use them as bait," I say.

"Do not."

"Can't keep them as pets, it's crewwwwel. You'll kill them anyway."

The girls will never leave now. I push out Mom's red canoe Dad gave her for her birthday but she's never used and probably won't. "Cost me a fortune," says Dad. I roll it over in the shallow water, come up underneath. Light bounces off the river bottom into its insides. Golden ripples on the ribs, not dark. My breath inside, louder than I've ever heard it. "Tomahawk," I whisper. Funny one person can make so much noise just being alive. But when I whoop and scream the sound

71

stops fast, faster than if you're not inside. I dip down and come out. "Did you hear me?"

"Hear what?" (Joycee never tells the truth, and she's 'vangelis Christian). "You're scaring the fish," she says, still snitty.

Now the moms have come down to the beach.

"When's lunch?" I shout.

"We're not hungry yet." Joycee snaps at me in a whisper.

"Mom?" I call. But they keep talking (Dad says gossip is women's work). I watch them from behind the canoe, can't stop thinking about what I heard them say about Tom's dad and his mom's nurse. And Mom acts different—more polite—when she's around Joycee's mom, calling out to us to "behave." She crosses her legs, too. Hands held as if she's praying. 'Course Joycee's mom has got some kind of connection with God and church camps, which we don't.

But they run back and forth between our places with recipes and cookies and baking and movie mags and paperbacks all summer long, like my family got bigger.

"You can stop giving her those movie mags," Dad told her.

"And why, pray tell?" Mom asked (whatever that means).

"I saw the whole lot of them in the garbage when I got the water yesterday. She just takes them to be polite."

Mom still gives them anyway, just in case Mrs. O'Brien wants a peek.

"Joycee," calls her mother, from the beach. "It's lunchtime dear."

"Lunch?" she shouts like a spoiled brat, sneers at me.

"Come along dear."

"Maaaahhhwther," wails Joycee. (Mother is Joycee's name for her mom—even when it's an emergency it's "Mother! Mother!")

So her mom pops up off the rock she was sitting on, says something to my mom about continuing their chat, and then goes up the path. Mom sits on the rock till Mrs. O'Brien is on her way.

"You kids get out of the water when I go up. I'm not having a drowning on my hands, not like that little retard."

"That was in the winter."

"And no back talk."

"Lunchtime Joycee," I say.

The screen door slams, which means her mom has gone inside. The screen doors are one of the sounds clear on the river, other than loons, tree frogs, cows on the other side, crickets and us. The whippoorwills at night. Not many motorboats. Not today, and since Mr. Whiteside had met his *gruesome* fate—as Mom calls it, growling the *r* part—there is one less. The Whitesides don't even put their boat in the river anymore—just sits on the shore like a big white tub it is, going rotten. Mr. Whiteside built it.

For all the back and forth, Mrs. O'Brien doesn't like the way me and Margaret are. She doesn't ever talk to us. She's

73

always watching from the top of that hill where their cottage is. If I skinny-dip she'll be up there, hands pointed to God. The blind'll be up. Thinks she knows what's best for me. She can't mind her own business. I can always tell when she's minding mine and looking at us out the window. I can feel it. Prob'ly because once Joycee made me laugh and I spit milk all over her mom, and then I burned Joycee with a flaming marshmallow and heard her mom say, if I ever catch you within a mile of those heavens or heathens or something.

"What's a heathen?"

"A bug," said Dad.

"What kinda bug?"

"A question-asking bug."

"Oh."

"For heaven's sake," Mom said to Dad—then, "Look it up in the dictionary."

"How do you spell it?"

"That's what a dictionary's for."

That makes no sense, and it can't be important anyway.

I plug around in the loosestrife and reeds, everything purple and green, till all the rocks are turned. Bright green slime on one side and after touching them your hands smell like the turtle bowl at school. Joycee's got no frogs but Margaret's gotten a jar of minnows. Wish they'd scat—for *heaven's* sakes.

"You stirred it up," I says.

"You made it muddy," says Joycee.

And she's off the board sending Margaret in a spin like she's caught in a whirlpool, till she rolls off, too.

"Water never used to be muddy," said Dad. "When I was a boy I could see the bottom, clear as glass. The Frenchies started dumping their garbage and *merde* into the river, changed the colour."

"Dad, you forgot, you're a Frenchie."

"You too, Dougaldo."

"Not all."

"Half potato-head."

"Does that make me half-breed like Tom?"

"Not like Tom."

There's no poop on our side, and the Frenchies are at least two miles away. It's the logs and the log booms, because after the tugboat goes by, the river is always all brown. Even if they poo, I think he made it up.

The tugboat chugs faraway forever and ever. Margaret drags the stuff—the yellow board, the net, the jar—onto shore. I hope they want lunch 'cause the tug is to the curve of the river, near the island, past Tomahawk's. Still it looks like it's not moving. If you don't look and look back, then magically it's moved. Logs never come until a long time after and then the boom just keeps coming and coming and it's not until late that it's out in front of the house.

I squint to see it move and then, some surprise, Tom's little boat catches my eye as it shoots out from his place. I wave hard. It's like last summer for me to see him come over. But the bratty girls are still on the beach. I drop the canoe on shore and run to the end of the dock and wave my arms. The boat circles wide before skimming back towards me.

"You're going to get it," sings Margaret. But it's Joycee's big mouth and not Margaret's that will tell. Tom brings the boat in slow. I look back at the girls, Joycee looking mean and Mrs. O'Brien with the blinds up. I don't say nothing, and get in the boat.

We speed out to the tug, me and Tom in his nine-horse. He doesn't talk.

"Don't you have to take care of your mom?" I say.

"Not today."

"Is there a nurse?"

"Doc Smiley's wife is the nurse."

"She takes care of your mom?"

"Except I have to watch the Smiley kids—Baby David and Huey," he says.

And as we head towards the tugboat, the log boom that it's pulling gets closer and closer, big arms wrapped around thousands of logs—like you could walk on the whole field of them.

"You ever wanted a brother?" I say.

"Like a baby brother?"

"No just a brother."

He just looks at me, like there's something behind me.

"Tom? Does your mom take her medicine?"

"I guess."

"What do you do when you take care of her?"

"Mostly just sit nearby when she's painting."

"What about today?"

"I'm not supposed to be around when she's not good."

"Oh."

Tom ties a lasso with ski rope. He tosses it towards a stray deadhead. The deadhead bobs up and down, the other end is a way, way down into the dark. We try to pull it backwards but it must be stuck in the bottom, so he loops a plastic bottle to the big slippery end of it.

"No one trying to poison your mom?" I say.

"Nope."

"Not Nurse Smiley?" I say.

"Your dad having an affair with his secretary?" he says back.

"Nope," I say.

"Then no one trying to poison my mom," he says.

We come up close to the boom and Tom puts his leg over the side and grabs with his spread toes, puts his bare foot on the boom, and flips out of the boat onto it. Leaves me. I know how to drive his nine anyway, if need be. He walks on the boom, arms like wings keeping his balance and every muscle in his back like smooth beach stones. It doesn't matter him walking on the boom 'cause the guy driving the tugboat is a mile away so can't do nothing. What's he going to do? Stop the tug? Tom says it takes days to stop the boom from moving. It's like an island with nothing under it. If you fell off you'd be looking up and seeing all them logs over your head, sun shining through the spaces making it all like golden curtains. Then you'd drown.

"Where's Baby David and Huey today?" I call to him.

"Doc Smiley took them to town."

He jumps back in the boat, and the floating island slowly drifts away from us, leaving currents and eddies behind on the dark water. It ripples like the skin on the back of Mom's legs.

Tom lets me drive us back to O'Briens'.

"See you later?"

He nods.

I run on the dock, making it bounce, and race upstairs, smiling till it hurts.

All the lunch stuff is gone. Pickles are back in the fridge and the sandwiches are wrapped in wax paper.

"That's the last you see of him," says Mom from out of the dark corner. Her cheeks are extra swollen and kind of red and I figure she must have been napping.

"We didn't do nothing."

"*Anything*, and don't argue, he's trouble, especially after what Joycee's mother told me."

"What?"

"Enough of your cheek. Besides…"

"Besides what?"

"It's high time you went to that Bible camp."

I can't stand what she says and I can't stand Mrs. O'Brien either. She's going to ruin our lives for the whole summer, if we let her.

My room is dark, even in daytime. Woods make it like that in summer. My pillow smells like pine trees, smells like that when it gets tears on it. Mom calls it *mildoo*. Anyways I sniff as quiet as I can so she can't hear me. Can't find a dry place to put my face on the pillow. And anyway it wouldn't matter if I didn't play with him at all. Tom prob'ly doesn't even know I'm alive when we aren't together. Mom said that about Dad.

SIX

I forgot she's in this film. Someone else is holding the camera. Her and Dad are sitting on the steps of the house, before me and Margaret came along. They're smiling and Dad looks proud with his arm squeezing Mom. He keeps moving her close to him. She'd hate it now if he did that.

"What's an addition?"

"A veranda," says Mom.

"A what?"

"A big porch."

"Money wasted," says Dad.

"So we won't roast on top of each other for another summer," says Mom. "And we won't get eaten alive when guests come up."

Every summer Dad has his office party and they all come for drinks, barbeque and swimming. Mostly we sit outside on picnic tables until we have to crowd inside.

So the workmen start building a veranda and Mom gets cranky, says it's the hammering.

Dad just goes to the office.

Mom pays more visits to Joycee's mom, and Dad gets up earlier every morning and then comes home sometime after we go to sleep.

"It's wearing on me," Mom says. "They're no longer babies."

All's I can see of her taking care of us is when she yells over her shoulder to quit picking on each other. Oh, and we have soup and sandwiches, too.

I think of Tom, back at home, with his mom or with the Smileys' Baby David and Huey, their long monkey faces, all whiny. I wish I had a boat. I could pull up to the end of his dock and take him away, and never stop 'cause it would be up to me. We'd go all the way up the river like the explorers, past the dam and all the way to North Bay.

There's a film of the front of the house with only the spruce and pine and the Pontiac, no people in it, but now the trees are being cut down to make room for the veranda.

Hot afternoon. Low cloud. The whole world is one smooth colour. You can't see the other side of the river. The workmen went early and, except for the tree frog's buzz in the heat, it's quiet. Mom and Margaret are napping. Tom's nine is idling quietly at the end of the dock. I pretend Joycee isn't around—if I even think of her then there she'll be. I sneak on tiptoe or I'll have to play with Margaret or sweep the workmen's sawdust off the floor or something. I don't care Mom said I can't see him. I know what a bad influence is and he's not. Not like Joycee's mom on mine.

I don't slam or even squeak the screen door, and then I scoot silently down the hill, knees bending extra to keep twigs and needles from snapping. Even so, I feel Mrs. O'Brien's big white face watching me and thinking I'm up to no good.

I don't even make the dock bounce. I step into the boat with not a word and sit facing Tom. He doesn't talk. His legs are open over the back seat of the boat and one of his nuts hang out.

Everything is still. The water is flat calm. You can't tell where the river stops and the sky starts. There's no breeze to make the grey go away, no thunder, nothing. The motor putt-putts 'cause we're trolling a line. We go east as far as where there is no beach, just rock. The wake from the boat and the fish line make the only waves on the water.

Closer to the bay, trees hang out over the rock ledge. A small cabin catches our eye probably because it's a shape you don't have in the woods. Most of the scenery is only trees shooting up.

"We can go there sometime," Tom says.

"Haunted," says I (but Tom looks at me sideways like it's a lie). "And even more than that there's this tunnel in it that goes to a barn way up the hill that you can't find anymore. Everyone's heard about it."

I look back. He grins like he knows the truth. His sac is still stuck to his leg. I look at his feet, too: wide, thick, with the edge whiter than the tops, like T-bones.

The haunted cabin is behind us now. There's more rock, less evergreen. A slanted meadow runs up to a grey stone house where it all flattens out, but the fog is still pushing down from behind. All's quiet until the line pulls, whizzes, then stops. Just a nibble, or maybe a snag. We putt-putt into the bay in front of us, long and narrow. There are cottages on both sides now and they're quiet, too, as if the whole world is taking a nap. We go all the way to the end. Reeds come up to meet the boat from the dark and scratch the bottom like chalk on the board at school. We turn around and head back out to open river.

Tom's knees are together. I can't see his bag anymore. His feet are pressed against the bottom of the boat. My toes are curled, barely touching the floor dirty with fish scales, dried out worms and shrivelled bait.

We head towards the middle, to the river at its widest. But with the fog there's nothing in any direction. Tom shuts the motor. We sit. Current bends the rod. I hang my head and arms over the front. But with the grey I can't see any reflection. My fingertips push out little ripples feeling bigger than my whole hands. It tickles if I do it light enough. The dark water isn't bothering me. Tom's here.

Weeds drift past like they floated from the shore or were on the propeller. But more and more of them float by and then weeds thick as a finger painting surround us and we're stopped in the swirl of them. We look at each other. They hush underneath us. Tom pulls up the motor, but it's already tugging—green, mossy and thick.

I won't breathe. I can't. I pinch my fingers under the edge. Tom looks at me, stretches his leg and presses his foot on top of mine. My heart whacks under my shirt and everything in my body whacks, too, even my brain. I keep looking at him. He must know. Finally I whistle out some air.

"You okay?" he says.

"Me?"

And now his sac has plopped back in his trunks and I can't see it no more. I don't want to look at his foot on mine in case he thinks I like it too much, or maybe that it bothers me, and takes it away. So I act like I don't really notice. Even so, it feels like a big warm sponge.

"You know about this place?" he says.

"Oh yeah."

"How?"

"My mom said that… well, I just heard about it from someone."

"How would she know? And anyway you can only find it by accident."

"Maybe Joycee's brothers told me. They said the voyageurs died here."

"Other people too," whispers Tom. "Especially if you get caught in it and panic." He presses his foot harder on mine.

"I never found it in all these years," I say.

"Got stuck here with Jimmy."

"You were out here with swim instructor Jimmy?"

Tom's toes twitch.

"You can't look for it," says Tom.

"Did you?"

"Nah. Jimmy and I found it by accident."

"In his big boat?"

But Tom says nothing.

"It's like the Sargasso Sea," I say.

He's still touching me. "What's that?" says Tom.

"Sargasso? We learned about it with the explorers. Not our voyageurs, though. More Columbus's guys."

He looks at me like I'm crazy talking about school.

"In the middle of the Atlantic Ocean. They get stuck in the Sargasso, no wind, sails all droopy, no current, nothing. Just all these ships there in this green seaweed, so thick, but you can't walk on it, and these sailors all hungry, starving in the heat, cracked lips, try to drink the salt water. The ships couldn't go, maybe never, and the sailors went crazy, ripped their hair out, or ate each other then died. Never made it to

85

those desert islands with the palm trees and coconuts. Never made it to paradise. I bet the Sargasso Sea is just like this, only bigger." Now I think I sound like a schoolteacher.

"They'd be scared," says Tom. "Are you scared?"

"If I was out here alone, without you, then I would be."

Tom puffs his cheeks and then pulls in the line. I can't shut up. "Injuns showed the white man up this river." Still Tom doesn't talk. "Weeds can be this long and it's not even August, I don't get it."

But he just looks at me, head tipped to one side.

"What if they were there all winter, the weeds, maybe frozen in the ice, so if you walk out far enough you might fall through right there and drown?"

Tom stares like he's wondering.

"What did you and Jimmy do here?"

He laughs a bit.

Mom's right, he does look Injun, I think—handsome. Thin wandering eyes, hair in them.

"Well?"

"I'm never scared," he says.

"I know," says I. "You ever hear of blood brother stuff?"

"Maybe."

"Say Injuns did it lots."

"Maybe they say it, but it's not true. Lots of things people like to think of Injuns. Like to think of my mom that way. Like she's an Injun. Like why she married Dad. It's not true. Anyway I'm not an Injun."

86

"Think you'd ever be a blood brother?" I say. Tom twists, looks into the water. "Think we'll ever find it again?"

"If we look for it," he says.

The shore is gone in the fog and now all we float in is grey, no part of the world.

"And if this is the Sargasso Sea, what's the Landing going to be?" Tom says.

"Africa maybe—it can be Africa."

"And the other side?"

"India or China. No, India. And the island can be Australia. Except…"

"Except what?"

"Except Dad says our whole country's history went up this river."

"Even if your old man says that, it can still be the Sargasso Sea."

"Sure Tom."

He peels his foot off of mine, leaving a dampness. Puts both his feet up on the side of the boat and leans back along the seat, hands folded on his stomach. I breathe in big, quiet so he can't hear—turn to look over the weeds—lean back. We look around. We look at each other. Mostly I look at him and his legs and feet hanging there. All is still. The whole world is still. There's a rumble of thunder, and even so, it's probably still a day away.

"Jimmy's got a nice boat," I say.

"Let's go back to Africa."

"Aye aye," says I, and we paddle ourselves out of the sea and back into the dark water, our river, that's more like the rest of the ocean if that was just the sea. Tom starts up the nine but keeps it slow and, as we putter, the Landing starts to show through the fog.

"That is definitely the last time," says Mom. "I almost called the police."

"Tom's dad is the police."

"Enough cheek."

"We were fishing."

"Fishing for trouble. Do you know what time it is?"

"How should I know? I never saw the sun."

"Joycee's mother told me. Do you know what can happen in that fog?"

The sky stays grey. The air is still and hot, like a room with no windows. Just the sounds of her making a fuss. "Savages," she says—I think she got that one from Mrs. O'Brien. Dad gets home and she finally stops talking. She's all wheezed out and can't work up the energy to tell Dad how bad I was. He couldn't care anyway. We eat cold Fancy Franks. No one talks, not even Margaret.

After dinner, a wind comes up and blows towards the thunder in the west and the storm comes in fast, like it's sucking the wind into it. It starts with pelts on the roof and then one burst like it was being flushed down on us. Margaret shoves her big bum between Mom and Dad.

I lie in my bed, watch the flashes off the ceiling and walls. I think about the Sargasso Sea: the weeds stirring in the dark under the sky, whipping foamy whitecaps, setting the sailors free, blowing the fog away. I pull the covers close. Tom is in the dark. He swims in the lightning whenever he wants, but now I think it's too late to be out in it, maybe it's early morning. I lie on my back and try to close my eyes but they open each time there's a flash so I close them again when it crashes. Why would he have gone out there with Jimmy?

I wish someone felt safe with me.

SEVEN

Joycee and me next day in the woods and we're not twenty steps from her place when we squat and poo through a hole in the dead cedar. Might be good for a toilet if we make a new fort. When I was younger I used to pee between her legs while she was sitting on her toilet. This is easier because we wipe up with leaves.

"You heard of blood brothers?" I say.

"What?"

"You know. Blood brothers. You should—'cyclopaedia says it's biblical."

"Maybe it is. I thought it was the Indians."

"Tom says…"

"What does Tom say?"

"Nothing. He doesn't know either."

"Even if I knew I wouldn't tell *you*."

After, when Joycee is having her lunch, I see Tom up on the road shooting stones into the woods, like he knows he's trouble as far as Mom and Mrs. O'Brien think. I take off on everyone quick and quiet again. Bite my lip 'cause I feel a smile coming on. He's got a plastic bag of wieners—buns, too—tied to his belt loop and it slaps on his leg while we walk. Margaret said Thierry had something to eat when he made blood brothers. We take the road up to the dead end where it stops in the woods and turns into a path.

"Where we going?"

He doesn't talk, and already I made too much noise with my words.

"The cabin?"

"Mmmm," says Tom.

"The one we saw from the water?"

But he doesn't say more, so I'm quiet, too.

The forest is dark and the trees thick, the ground crunchy with dried needles. It's all like the forest around Sleeping Beauty's castle before the prince came. Branches of trees reach out to grab us. No matter how much wind there is up on the road, the forest is still and quiet like that. We walk further into the dark till we see flashes of the river through the trees. The point of the roof of the empty cabin looks the same as when we saw it from the boat. So down we go.

Windows are boarded with planks but the door is open. A yawning face with closed eyes. Tom goes in first. The door

91

squeaks. A bonfire of feathers and candles are stuck on the floor, and a flat mattress on a rusty frame is shoved in the corner.

"Maybe we shouldn't be here."

Tom doesn't say anything.

"Mom says places like this collapse on kids all the time and they get trapped or just die."

"Your mom's an idiot."

He's prob'ly right.

I think of us there someday when everyone else is grown up and gone and all's I have to do is make our food and rub his feet and he can go fishing for dinner. Then we can do the ceremony.

Quiet.

My nose whistles when I breathe. Tom walks around the candle pile, tight-roping each step.

Matching china plates with little bluebirds kissing each other stand on the shelf. He reaches out to one of the plates and pats it on his hand.

"Do you want to eat the wieners now?" I say. If two people feed each other—I feed him and he feeds me—then that's the first part of the blood brother ceremony.

But I jump 'cause he smashes the plate hard on the floor. It barely breaks so he wings it at all the others making them bowling pin off the shelf but they only break a little. I do the same. Then he collects all the plates and goes outside and shouts and smashes plate after plate after plate on the rock ledge making a pile of pieces.

I plug my ears and think someone might hear. And all of a sudden there is nothing left to smash, so he pushes the broken pieces around with his feet. Then it's quiet. Tom grins when he looks at the ground.

I pick up some of the bigger chunks and go back in the house and lean them on the shelf. They don't look nice anymore. I pick up some of the other pieces, wonder if anyone could match them. I try to make the birds kiss again but I can't, so I pile them by the door. Put some in my pocket.

Down at the shore, he's skipping pieces into the river.

"Maybe we shouldn't have done that," I say.

"Only sissies *don't* do stuff," he says.

He crouches down by the shore, pulls up a frog by its back legs and goes back to the house. I decide to build a fire. He comes back with a plank and tosses the frog into the air and bats it. The frog makes a plopping sound and then pinwheels out over the water—arms and legs all out trying to fly before it splash-lands. Little ripples start up in the water, and you know it's still alive and pretty stupid, too, because it's swimming in for another whack.

"Grab one."

"No."

"You did it last summer."

"So?" I pretend to be busy and set a place for a fire up on the ledge by the river. I pile red and brown cedar twigs from

93

the forest bottom that burn quick. I get it going good. I can do that.

Tom comes and sticks some of the weenies on a branch, and then leaves them too close to the flame. They're just starting to blister when I take them off. We eat, watching the fire while it twists this way and that. He goes away again, finished with hitting frogs and then comes back with this metal bowl, dips it in the river, fills it, and sets it on the flames. Soon bubbles start to spring off the bottom. We dunk a weenie just to boil it and then Tom whips out his own weenie and there's even some hair and he starts to pee, clear not even yellow, and it sizzles by the fire. Then he just pees in the pot of bubbling water, so there's pee boiling now. I unzip, too, but can't squirt. He's watching me anyway, and mine isn't as hairy. As a matter of fact, no hair.

When Tom tucks it away, I do, too, and he grabs one of his stunned frogs from the shore, just breathing in his hands all calm. He drops it in the boiling pee and the frog only jerks a bit and then its skin spreads and splits till there's this white stuff. I gag my wieners into the back of my throat. One frog isn't enough so he pokes around on the shore and pulls up this fat bullfrog, all bright green, from between a crack in the ledge.

That's when I grab for it and him. He's squeezing it and so am I and I let go my grip in case I squish it. But I dig my fingernails into his arm, and he laughs but drops it, even though he could have kept hold of it. I toss it out into the water

94

but it wants to swim back to shore, so I stand between Tom and it, splashing towards the frog and then at Tom, back and forth, back and forth, until he finally gives up on it. He laughs again, and with this grin on his face comes at me and shoves me hard. The air goes out of me and I fall back.

"Even girls kill frogs," he says.

But I don't care anymore 'cause I see an old guy sitting where we smashed the plates. I figure he heard everything—the screaming and smashing. This must be the old hermit I heard about a long time ago. He stares at us, his wrinkly face turned down, looking half sad and half like he couldn't care. So we take off, run as fast as we can, along the long flat rocks. Tom passes me in seconds—even so, I try to keep up. Besides, I'm mad. Funny to see him run ahead like he's scared. Maybe he just wants me to know he can run faster than me.

When we slow down I scratch this itch in my crack. Can't stop.

"What?" Tom says.

"Nothing."

"You look funny."

"Just itchy."

"Let's see."

It doesn't matter he looks at my bum, he's seen it before lots when we changed swimsuits at his place.

"Maybe there's prickles in my pants." I drop my drawers and bend over and Tom has a look.

"Poison ivy."

"No way."

"Yes way."

"Oh geez, wiping up with Joycee."

"What?"

"But I *know* what it looks like—three leaves."

"What?"

"Me and Joycee pooed in the woods."

"You like playing with girls?"

"All's we did was poo."

"Sissy."

"You smashed the dishes. You boiled that frog in pee!" I say.

"Why don't you run home, tell your mommy?"

"Maybe you got a problem."

"Yeah, you. Go play dolls with Joycee."

I pull up my drawers and take off up the hill without looking back at him, even if I want to. Last time he gets to look at my bum.

The lotion stings when I dab. I try to be quiet in the bathroom so no one hears. Put the cap on the counter real quiet and no one's going to know because someone always has poison ivy. Bottle's always out. The lotion doesn't help much.

I go to get water and Joycee is outside, but she won't say nothing about being itchy to me. I bet she thinks God made it happen. I don't know if it's 'cause I took off on her or 'cause she got the poison ivy, too.

"You roll in the poison ivy with Joycee O'Brien?" says Mom.

"Nope."

"Mrs. O'Brien says so."

"She's a fat liar."

Mom doesn't say anything 'cause I think she thinks Mrs. O'Brien is a fat liar, too.

"Heard you were down to MacLaren's," says Mom.

"MacLaren who?" Maybe he was the old guy who watched us wreck the cabin.

"Kids die in them abandoned buildings all the time. Just happened down the river a few weeks ago. Little boy and his sister squashed. Barn fell right on them."

She doesn't say more about it but just looks at me, eyebrows raised. She never looks at me otherwise. "Mrs. O'Brien told us about a summer camp they sent Joycee to before."

"Not this year," I try to whine. "Camp is never fun."

"In August. Two weeks, while your father and I go away."

"I'm not going."

"We'll see what your father says."

I go to my room and try not to cry, 'cause I know they want me to go—and I still feel Tom's push into the water—and maybe he is a bastard.

EIGHT

After swim lessons some of us gather together: Big Red, Joycee,
Baby David and Huey, who Tom has to keep an eye on, but no
Margaret this time.

"Where are you going?"

"Don't know."

"Not back to that shack."

"Don't know."

"Take your sister," says Mom.

"Why?"

"There's no kids her age down at this end."

"She's too young."

"You'll take her."

"Dad doesn't take you everywhere."

While she and Margaret are quiet from what I just said,
I take off with the grub and boiled eggs I snatched from the

fridge. I don't feel good about what I said now. I won that one too easy. I head up the path into the woods with the others.

"Where's your sister?" says Tom, more like he's making fun of me.

I don't say anything.

This time I have to share him and I figure there's going to be no alone stuff, not this time, not ever. He doesn't care if I come anyway. He leads us because he does his own exploring. I swat blackflies from my head, reach at my bleeding ankles ripped because of brambles, thistles and thorns. Try to keep up. From time to time we come up to the barbed fence running through the forest and maybe it was put there a hundred years ago, and then we pass the low cedar brush that helps mark our way. We keep going up until finally we come to a flat rock wall about four times as high as me, straight up, and jutting out of the side of the hill. Tom gets on his knees and disappears under this ledge and one by one everyone does.

"After you, Big Red."

"*Chicken Little*."

She can say what she wants but I just don't want to be stuck with no way out if she gets wedged behind me.

No one has candles, no flashlights. It's all dark when I duck in. The ceiling gets lower until I have to crawl with my elbows on tiny sharp stones in a stream. My front is wet, and my face is on the ground so I can't barely breathe. I feel like I'm still going up a hill, but I'll explode if it doesn't end soon. Even if I can go back I can't wait much longer to see daylight. But Big Red moves ahead and I finally see a slice of blue sky.

"Dougaldo make it?" Tom says.

I stand up straight out of the hole and put up my eyebrows high, like Joycee does, and I look right at him. We're on top now, and you can see how wide the river is. It's at least two miles from the Frogs, the French Frogs, and the hills from here look like mountains. It's all different. From the shore down by the water the river doesn't look like this. From the shore it's flat. Now the mountains on the other side aren't grey as much as greens on the bottom and blues on top. The greens are hills with farms and fields and fences, and the blues, mountains, the Canadian Shield, all rock with little lines of trees growing along them here and there. I can see how wide the river really is. Sandbars poke out from the shore by the bay where it's lighter, and from one part that's darker. That must be the Sargasso Sea. That's where we got stuck, together. In the middle. Where his foot pressed on mine. Seems impossible that it will happen again.

Blue sky reflects in water, except in the Sargasso Sea. It can make you lonely, all that space. Past that, on the French side you could wander anywhere in those mountains forever and never be found.

Joycee cozies herself up to Tom. Every time he turns around she's right there, in her shorts, and lines squeezing the skin around her chest from her tube top. Girls are pests and she's growing these little titties that she tries to touch him with

I'm sure. But she'll never see the Sargasso Sea. He'll never show her that—they'd never get out in his boat without her mom having a fit. *She'll never see the Sargasso Sea*, goes over and over in my head like a tune. Na, na na na naaaa naaaa.

He walks ahead, her near him. Down we go, down the hill and to the pond which we missed on the way up. They say the middle of the pond is bottomless, but that's never been proved. How could you prove it anyway? And little dots are making ripples on the pond. Turtles shove their heads to the surface for air and then disappear if one of us moves or even breathes. So I throw a stone and all the little heads vanish, leaving pockets of circles even where you didn't think they were.

He and Joycee look at me at the same time, like I'm stupid, or annoying—like Mom would do.

"At least I didn't try to kill them."

We go 'round the pond and up past the dungeons—two big holes in the ground with stone walls and animal bones in the bottom like they fell in and couldn't get out—but we've been in them before. So we go to an old barn in a clearing, go in and make ourselves comfy in the cool hay in the loft. We eat our picnic food, Joycee beside Tom giving mean looks at me whenever I look at them. She knows I'm laughing at her titties.

"Father says blood brothers are in psalms." She says this like a know-it-all.

I look at Tom, then her. "*Saw-ums*."

I hope here that she'll choke or drop dead 'cause my face is gone cold, but she keeps right on like her mom, or mine. "And I know which one."

"What's saw-ums, anyway?"

"It's a book. In the Bible."

Now I know she's just talking foolish. I look at Tom.

"Dougaldo ask you about blood brothers?" she cheeps.

Tom looks at me.

I can't eat any more eggs after that. I pitch the whites and eat the yellows. It makes me sick, her talking like that. Makes me miss Margaret. I wonder if she misses us. Now she's my only friend. Not wanting her here is like throwing stones at Doc Smiley's fat dog to keep it from following us all the time. Only difference is we don't throw stones at Margaret.

Then I hear an engine and wonder why. So far in from the main road, only way here is through the graveyard and it's gated up. But when I look between the boards I see a pickup truck bouncing across the clearing, and farmers waving rifles and shouting.

"Run!" is all I can say and it feels good to get something out and we're down from the loft, out of the barn and racing, the half-breed miles ahead of any of us now, including Joycee. I'm happy seeing her filled with as much scaredness as the rest of us. Look at the two of them, running like fools. We pass the pond and connect up with the cedar bushes, then the fence, and finally the path out of the forest, catching our breath.

I'm guessing old man Fitzroy had it with us making a playground of his property.

I leave Joycee alone with Tom. Other than saying my bedtime prayers I never pray, except now I pray her mom finds out.

At home the veranda is finished. Mom set up cots on it for Margaret and me next to the screen, and that night after we say our prayers we lie side by side, closer to nature than we ever have been.

"Where do you go with Tom?" she says.

"Lots of places."

"Is it dangerous?"

"Not really."

"Joycee go too?"

"Nope."

"What's he like?"

"Quiet."

"Is he your best friend?"

"Sometimes. Once we went to a place called the Sargasso Sea and it was all green and quiet and you could see the weeds moving down below but we didn't move at all—I wasn't scared."

But she's fallen asleep.

"Now I lay me…" I say and this time I pray I'll never be mean to her again, which I know is impossible but for now I don't want to feel as bad about losing Tom to Joycee.

NINE

On the movie screen is me looking even more like a girl, standing there in clam diggers and no kind of shirt for a boy to wear. I'm holding a bass on the line all by myself even though you know someone else is not in the scene but helping 'cause I jump every time it flips. Maybe it's one of the ones they say I kept in a bucket for a pet.

I'm itching to catch whatever kind of fish tried to swallow my toe last summer. That's something I'll never forget. I'm not a fisherman. Tom the half-breed and Mr. O'Brien, Joycee's dad, have it in their blood. I get busy wasting time or teasing Margaret and then I see they been down at the water for a long while casting out or just sitting by the rod. That's how you make fisherman's luck.

He touched me on my face. Tom. Once I was casting out and the lure caught on the edge of the dock and then flicked off and hooked the skin under my eye. He made me lie on my back, pressed my forehead with his rough hand and his other palm against my face, fingers on his jackknife, blade brushing at the hook. He was so close, so still, warm breath on my face. Mom would have stopped me from more fishing, probably tell me I'd put my eye out. Her favourite warning.

On the dock, orange sun is surrounded by purple, sinking behind the island. Wind stops as always at this time, before it blows back out from the farmers' fields, warm across the water. Dinnertime for the fish. I don't know if I have the luck those guys have but my line is in the same place where old man O'Brien always puts his. Mom is up at the house clinking bowls and pots, Dad not home yet, and Margaret with her sticker book. No sound from O'Briens'. Probably she is reading the Bible. We don't have one. At least if we do I don't know where. No need if we say our prayers anyway.

Everything's quiet. If Tom thinks I'm a sissy he can play with Baby David and Huey all summer long. No sign of him at his dock, maybe with his mom. No one wondering where I am. I wish it could be like this forever, knowing they're there but not having to be around them, to throw sand or pull anyone's hair, just sit and watch the sun shoot over the island. Not fight for Tom as if it's all that matters. I bet Tom thinks sunsets are all that matters.

The rod is inching back and forth like it can't make up its mind, just teasing whatever's down there. Come on, little fishies, come on. Dinnertime, juicy worm, tastier than a lure. Bingo! Rod curves towards the water and the float's gone for good. I'm up, grab the rod fast before it flies, and I wind on the line. "I caught a fish! I caught a fish!" I scream to the beach. Rusty gears squawk back at me.

Someone shoots out from the bushes at the foot of O'Briens' beach. I think it's going to be Doc Smiley's dog, but then I see it's Tom. And he's out onto the dock, and it bounces when he walks, trampolines when he starts to run. The line runs back and forth along the bottom and the float follows. He grabs the rod from me. His arms stringy and tight when he reels against it. I don't mind he has the line. He fights it, back and forth. I watch him, but pretend to be looking to the water. Some branches crackle and I look around and the bushes shake again, where Tom was, and it's Joycee who stumbles out.

"Catfish," he says.

She knows I seen her. "Boney," I say, looking back at him.

"Not if you clean it right," says she, coming up the dock.

I know they were doin' something and it sure wasn't pooing through a log.

He pulls the line around the side of the dock, grabs it. Hauls up a long shiny thing. Not a catfish. More like I caught the pumphouse hose. But it twists and coils to get back to the water, as if there's no bone in its shiny black skin. It's thick,

106

too, like those tree roots over the rocks. I couldn't wrap one hand around it.

"It's the eel," says Joycee. "You caught the eel!"

"Tried to swallow my foot last summer."

"Must be three-feet long," says Joycee.

I ignore her. "I could keep it," I say to Tom.

"As a pet?" Tom says, squinting.

"As proof."

"Too big for the bucket," says Tom.

"Eat it," Joycee says.

"Kill it?"

"Can't let it die in a bucket," says Tom.

"Throw it back, I don't care. It's what tried to eat my toe, and who knows what next—and swimming around with that snake…"

Joycee doesn't talk.

Tom squeezes the head and grinds the hook from its mouth. Metal on bone and the eel gagging. It's around the jaw good and hard until he jerks it. Then, quick, he rolls it into the water, before I can stop him. It floats for a second then snakes away. Now I'll have to be brave forever.

"You can go back to the bushes," I says and Joycee opens her pie-slit eyes wide like she's going to say something. "You're slippery as that fish. Tell your mom I said that."

Next day I show up at Tom's with O'Briens' Bible.

"What do you got?"

"Joycee's Bible."

"Why?"

"Just to borrow it."

"Why?"

"To make the blood brother ceremony."

"What's a Bible got to do with that?"

I just shrug 'cause he'll see. I can borrow their Bible. Landing folk can do that. Besides O'Briens have nearly all Mom's movie mags. I wrap the Bible in my towel. Now we can be brothers, except that the bratty little neighbours, Doc Smiley's monkey-face kids, are there for Tom to watch, so I'm a tag-along and brothers'll have to wait.

It's Tom's idea to take the brats to the island and go fishing, so we take the wooden rowboat—not the nine, it needs gas—out to the middle and row hard against the current for what seems like an hour until we're over the sandbar at the island. We paddle, but have to walk the boat when it's too shallow. Golden sand and bright yellow reeds scratch at the bottom of the boat as we wade through the channel that cuts the island in half. Then we hop in and row over the deeper water. In here no one can see you from the river.

There's more reeds and new lily pads starting out along the edges and big old trees hanging over the water. It looks like those pictures of the Congo or the Amazon from the magazines with the bare-skin Africans all running around and alligators, too. We chuck the rope high to a branch but it doesn't catch so Tom shinnies, hands pulling and feet like hands holding the trunk, all the while with the rope in his teeth. And when he's down, his skin is red with specks of blood and bark. I grab my towel and heave it, but forget the Bible's there and it fans open and then plops into the water, floats for a second and then it sinks away.

We both look at where it went in. O'Briens'll never know I took it. Good I didn't ask them, after all. "We'll get it after," Tom says. He rubs the towel over the red dots on his arms.

We stand on shore with the rope then run and swing out over the water and let go when we're high enough to splash into the channel. Mom said kids have hanged themselves playing with rope, but I don't want to tell Tom anything more about what she says.

After that, Tom disappears into the dark water and when he comes up he heaves the muddy Bible into the boat. It doesn't look like a Bible anymore, more like a dead muskrat, which I thought it was at first. It smells like one, too. Now I don't know what I'll say. Wish he didn't find it. Maybe I can fix it, wash it and dry it—it'll dry in the sun, I hope.

Anyway, today we're going to catch as many little perch as we can and take them back to the turtle pond. They flash around the end of the boat, yellow and silver over the sand. Tom puts bits of clam on the hooks—makes me gag 'cause it looks and feels like snot. We drop them over the side of the boat. Fish poke at the bait. I get a nibble and yank on the line too hard for a baby fish and it goes flying over the boat.

We laugh so I yank it again and the little fish flies out of the water, this time over our heads about twenty feet, and ends up hanging in the swinging tree. I pull to try to get it down but the harder I do, the tighter the line gets and the fish gets more stuck. I could break the line but Tom pulls out his red jackknife, snaps the line and we leave the fish bobbing over the water. People going to wonder how a fish got up a tree. All in all, we end up with about twenty-five baby perch scooting around in the bucket, minus a hook and some line.

When a good wind is up, we push back out of the channel. Wind's from the west so we tie a towel to the oars and sail like Vikings from the island to the Landing. The boat rides the swells and then dips, rides then dips. Except for some steering, we just let nature take us all the way back. No Sargasso Sea on the way.

"To hell with the Bible," I say when we unpack our loot. Tom just shrugs, so we leave it in the boat and head into the forest towards the turtle pond, me behind Tom and the brats behind me. Tom's arm's all hard, veins again, from holding the pail and leaning away so as not to let it splash too much. He tilts funny when he walks, the moving water making him sway. Straight hair slaps against his head. In bare feet, too—if the barbs and grass bug him he doesn't say. He's good at being brave. We take the path by the fence around the cedars and magically end up again at the pond. I could find it if I had to.

Baby David's gone, all of a sudden, and Huey starts to whine. But we can't go back till we dump the fish.

110

"Baby David's just gone home," says Tom. "Always does it. Stop crying Huey." Huey stops crying. Tom turns to me. "Does whatever I say. Watch. Take off your shirt Huey," says Tom.

Huey takes off his shirt.

"Throw it in the water."

Huey throws it in the water. Of course all the turtles disappear. And his shirt just floats there on the green stuff, it doesn't sink.

"Take off your shorts Huey," I say.

Huey takes off his shorts, just little white undies on.

"Stand in the pond," I say.

Huey walks slow into the water. Face scrunched up.

"Take off your undies Huey," I say.

He does, and throws them into shore where they land in the mud, all the while with that screwy face. But now he starts to cry and we stop laughing.

"Stop crying Huey," says Tom.

But Huey doesn't obey this time.

Soon Baby David shows up being carried by his mom, nurse Smiley. Her in her shorts, and long face looking like a monkey too, only prettier, slapping at mosquitoes while she shouts at us. How did a mom find the pond?

Nurse Smiley gives us all heck, but mostly the brats. "As if I don't have my hands full with that dying woman…" But we don't hear what will happen because Huey is crying and we're looking stupid and in trouble so we take off crackling through

111

the woods. It's not a place grown-ups know about and Baby David gave it away. We circle back and peer through the trees to make sure they're gone before coming out again into the clearing by the pond. Huey's shirt still stuck in the scum.

"Your mom dying?"

"Nope."

"You hate them?"

"Nope."

"You sure she isn't poisoning your mom?"

I guess I said too much 'cause I get the feeling Tom's going to explode.

"No more babysitting I guess."

"Wasn't babysitting," says Tom.

"Paid ya."

"Did not."

"Shoulda then."

"It's your fault," he says to me.

We grab the fish by their tails to chuck them one by one into the pond. Tom starts and I follow, throwing them high as we can before they splash-land and flip under the water. I wonder if the fish know where they've gone.

"You'll catch typhoid playing in that filth," says Mom. "Already been three cases of it in the bay this summer."

"It's only a pond."

"If Tom told you to jump in it, would you?"

I don't say. I put the towel with Tom's blood flecks under my pillow.

"The camp is called Gethsemane. Joycee's mom says there's space for you in August." She says this looking over her shoulder, barely enough to see me.

In my head I say I'm not going. "You said last summer was my last summer for camp."

"That's not true."

"All's we did at that frontier camp was play tetherball. Them kids all bored with not being in the city."

"You swam all the way across the lake and you learned French."

"Run by that crazy English lady—walked through the camp every morning while we were still asleep, singing, *Bowjour les gar, bowjour les fee, bowjour, bowjour, bowjour,* till it drove us crazy. Plus I'm no good at fighting kids."

"She said your French improved."

"Like you care! And I always have to sleep in a piss-stinking sleeping bag!"

"Stop yelling or they'll hear you clear over to O'Briens'," Mom says.

"*You're filthy*—that was the first thing you said when you seen me."

"Well she says this camp is different."

"Is Joycee coming too?" says Margaret.

"She's too old. Besides, they're making her a counsellor next summer. She'll have an honest-to-God real job."

Next day we're back at the pond, I'm wading around with a net while Tom's pulling turtles out. I'm trying to find Huey's shirt to say I'm sorry, but I can't find it at all. Any perch that wasn't eaten by turtles are now dead and belly up at the top of the pond. "No oxygen," says Tom.

We take the bucket of turtles now and head back from the pond to the island and into the channel to let the turtles go. They'll be way happier in the river.

Day after that, Mr. O'Brien wheezes as he takes us down to show us the catch of fish he'd wired up, alive in the water, been eaten, all of them, except for their heads, by a big turtle. "Heard about the turtles?" he says, hair looking like he slept standing on his head.

"But there were too many," I say.

"Where?" he asks.

"In the pond."

"So it's you boys in charge of nature. What do you think ate my fish?"

"Too big to be one of ours," I say.

Then he cuffs me up the side of my head.

"Tattle Joycee," I say to Tom.

Still, Mr. O'Brien doesn't know their Bible is gone.

TEN

We're hiking single file on the path that ends up near the ball diamond across from Madeline's. Tom has his BB gun, and he's brought some older guys along from farther down the Landing: Greasy Greg with his long hair; Bobby, a pimply Indian guy; and Don, with peach fuzz and whiteheads. I hang back.

We go through the brush to a clearing. Tom shoots at a rotten post and then some treetops. The other guys take turns, and then do what they like more than shooting guns, and that's to pull out cigarettes and start smoking.

"Lemme try," I say. The guys think it's the cigarettes I want, but Tom knows me.

"It's loaded." He shoves it in my hands.

I peek through the sight and stop when I see a blue jay just sitting on the ground, wings wide. The little black site crosses its body and I pull on the trigger too quick and it pops and

115

shoves my shoulder. The blue jay flutters in circles in the grass. Wings up, and they start shivering. First time I ever shot a gun, and all them guys watching and I think I hit the target.

"Why'd you do that?" Tom says.

"What?"

"Have to kill it now."

We walk to where it's flapping; the side is blasted open to the sky. Red blood on blue feathers and ribs showing, too. Half the bird is normal but the other half a quivering mess.

"Kill it," says Tom.

"Like you killed the frogs?" I say.

"Finish it off."

"No."

Tom snatches the gun and points it down at the crazy bird. I squat with my hands over my ears and he steps hard on what's left of it and holds the gun and shoots into its head. Covering my ears makes no difference.

It's dead now. He's right, why did I do that? But then I hear a louder shot, not from Tom's gun and look around to see an old guy limping fast towards us, waving his gun in the air. Prob'ly Fitzroy again.

"He's shooting salt," says Tom, then he shouts for us to run. But the other guys already took off.

"Bastard got me last summer," says Tom as we run.

"Why won't he leave us alone? Him and his stupid salt gun." I bet Tom can't hear a word I'm saying.

We tear into the woods until we're far enough to get our breath. Catch up to the other guys. Everything's still now and thunder rumbling. It could hit anytime. Back on the road, big drops of water smack us, with lots of time in between, like huge bird plops.

"See you guys," I say.

"Not comin' swimming?" says Bobby.

"His mom won't let him swim in the rain," Tom says. "Dougaldo's a momma's boy. Still wets his bed."

"Not anymore."

"Go take a shower. Homos take showers," Greasy Greg says. Tom doesn't say anything else. He started their meanness, so they can all go to hell. I keep going up the road till they turn into Tom's place. When they're gone I run back to the path. Rain starts heavier.

I cross the ditch and run back towards the baseball diamond across from Madeline's. I can't see. Tears are burning my eyes. My legs sting from the nettles when I take a wrong turn, and my itchy poison-ivy bum is burning in my shorts and I think I'm practically lost until I come out at the diamond. Coast is clear of old man Fitzroy and I find what's left of Mr. Blue Jay, getting pelted by the rain.

I pick up the tip of the one good wing. All of it there, attached like thread and strings, almost dragging on the ground when I walk. Still don't see the crazy farmer so I'm back into the woods, even faster this time since thunder's starting to crack. Mr. Blue Jay swings, sometimes hits my leg, but stays in one piece.

I have to be careful no one sees me back home. I crawl under the veranda with one of the coffee cans Dad keeps his nails in. I dump them out—doesn't matter they're all rusty now and forgotten by him. I pull two feathers off Mr. Blue Jay's wing and stick what's left of the bird in the can and then I sit back, under the edge of the new veranda, catch my breath before I go inside.

Later the storm steamrollers over Baird's Landing, shaking the ground under us. Margaret and me sealed up in the heat on either side of Mom, and we can't even go on the veranda to watch. If I am a homo, or a momma's boy, it's because she won't let me do anything fun.

"What a way for us to die," says Mom.

Meanwhile Tom's probably out to the raft swimming in the lightning and thunder, feeling the warm rain and seeing the lightning so close. He's probably jumping off the raft, his feet tucked up underneath—cannonballing, screaming, shoving, wrestling and laughing while we sit here. I think of Mr. Blue Jay, with no home to go back to, no parents, maybe children wondering what happened to him. What happened to their dad? He's dead in a can. Is this the way momma's boys think?

ELEVEN

"Wildlife suffers from *you*," growls Dad, teeth flashing, when he hears about the turtles. Did he find Mr. Blue Jay, too? How about the Bible? But we suffer sometimes, too, rolling in the poison ivy. It's all a big fat sin and we're punished—more itchy than normal because Mrs. O'Brien called on God.

In the film there's me in my genuine cowboy outfit: pants, vest, hat and pistols. None of that kid stuff fits now. My back to the camera and I go into the bushes fearless 'cause it protects me from everything like it would a real cowboy.

Since the veranda's finished, there's a new place for me to go hide. It's all up on blocks and lots of space above ground which means I can fit under, easy. No one can notice. I have my stash of comics and my candy from Madeline's. It's a real fort, small like the snow forts in the winter. Maybe it will be a good place for us to do the blood brother ceremony.

"You'll die of claustrophobia," says Mom about the winter forts. "Or worse, a cave-in." Sometimes I think she'd be glad to be rid of us.

So I've ducked under 'cause Margaret's crying. I knocked her fingers into the new electric fan by accident. Mom says I could've amputated her whole hand. It didn't do much more than surprise her. Even so, she had to cry.

I crawl low, with the wooden spoon in one hand, and duck away from nails sticking out from above. I look for soft ground and dig a hole with the spoon, to bury Mr. Blue Jay. The can fits into the hole and you can barely tell what's in it now. I cover it over.

The "*Jesu Crees*" nails poke my head from through the floor above. Then I feel a pinch from below, in my knee on the plank where some nails are sticking up, and on one of those nails is my knee. I can't move it. But I know it's going to hurt real soon. I call for Dad pretending it's not an emergency. If Mom knows, then I'm in for it. "Dad, Dad, Dad, Dad…"

The porch creaks above me, like small echoing steps far away. "Where the hell is he?" he says.

"Under here." Now he must know I'm in trouble because of the words and not how I say them. Steps run away on the porch and then the door slams and he's on the stairs. My knee twinges where the nail is, but still no blood, just the plank stuck to my knee.

His white legs come along the edge of the porch looking like stilts with no one on them. He crouches until I can see all of him.

"You under there?" he says as he ducks. He tries to wiggle towards me and whacks his head on the nails, too. Our arms reach to each other and then his big hands clamp onto my shoulders and he pulls. The board is still nailed to my knee, and now stinging into my whole leg. I scream and the tears wet my cheeks.

"*Jesu Crees!*" he says when he sees I'm attached to the board. But out he pulls me, slow, board and all.

"How the hell?" he says. He relaxes a minute and I pull my leg around. Feels like the knee part isn't just nailed to the board but nailed to the leg part, too. I can't move any of it.

"*Mer-de*," he says when he sees it. He holds me in his arms, my wet face in his shoulder till I turn to look. He pulls the board and the nail. It squeaks. He twists it and it squeaks more. I squeeze him hard. He pulls again and it groans like when you pull it out of wood. And out it comes and there's no hurt, just more like an ache. No blood either, only a little brown hole where the ruddy thing went in, and my tears.

Even Tom would think I'm pretty brave. And Dad's a hero now. He keeps holding me tight and boy do I cry like everything I tried to be nice to Tomahawk for and Tomahawk doesn't care. Dad holds me like he used to and no one does now, no hugs, nothing, makes me cry. He thinks it's the knee.

"Can I at least have my spoon back?" Mom pulls the spoon I dug the blue jay's hole with from my fingers. The crying is over when I have looks from her. She says she had "no idea," as if it was her fault. "Get him to the hospital before he dies of malaria."

"Tetanus," Dad says.

"That Bible camp will do him some good," she says.

Dad sticks me in the car for a needle at the hospital and Margaret comes running, blonde bangs flapping, wide eyes shiny with tears. Her dirty fingers stick a butterscotch Life Saver in my hand. If she hadn't seen me crying, I'd have told her about it anyways. But no one else.

Dad drives, doesn't talk, probably just thinking newspaper stuff like always.

"Is it the same hospital you took Mr. Whiteside to?"

"Took him to the city."

"But city's farther."

"He was too bad for town."

"He died anyway?"

"Died anyway."

Dad makes a phone call at the hospital. "Work," he tells me. I get a needle from an old nurse, rough hands and a voice that matches. She bandages my knee, and I get ice cream at the drugstore. I can't wait to show everyone the bandage—it's way bigger than the hole. They don't have to know about the hole or the tears. On the way home Dad's whistling, which he only does when he's real happy, which hasn't been for a while.

Other accidents happen other times. Grabbing a gray-hot coal I thought was a stone. "I snatched you off the ground and into the bathroom, stuck that white hand in a sink of cold water," says Mom. "I'm still surprised you didn't lose it."

"Really?" says Margaret.

"And then last summer that half-a-broken pop bottle," says Mom. "Sliced your foot open like meat." As usual Mom talks like she was there, but she wasn't. She was with Margaret up at Madeline's.

"I'll never figure out why you didn't go to O'Briens' for help."

"Didn't want her saying stuff…" (Truth is I was in my birthday suit.)

"To who?"

"To God."

"Like what?"

"About my foot—what does bless you and mercy me something mean anyways?—and me not understanding."

"My goodness—first time we've talked at the dinner table in a long time," says Mom.

We stop after that because none of us is for sure about bless you and mercy me. Mom frowns to herself.

There's still little scars on my foot now, like evidence of what I did, but not like Joycee's when we were roasting marshmallows. I flicked a flaming marshmallow on her arm. Instead of running to the river, she ran all the way up the hill to her place. Curls bouncing, her wailing.

"See what he did?" she sneered. "That's from his marshmallow. He slapped me with it, melted it into my arm." She always has to tell someone.

The film flickers and there's us with our marshmallows on little metal forks in the yard even before the barbeque was built, and not cooked marshmallows either, we think that's how it's done.

Even so, we *always* put ourselves in danger, mostly not knowing it unless Mom tells us how bad it could have been. "Against the odds," she likes to say. You can't think of it like Mom does or you will do nothing but stay inside. But it's accidents like the one that happened at Whitesides', and the boat running over and over the dad. That makes me careful. Tom doesn't care. I think we have warnings along the way: nail in the knee, glass in the foot, hot coals, Sargasso Sea. They say take care.

TWELVE

Now that the veranda is finished, all of the people they invite over in the summer, from town and city, get to sit on it. Mom watches us less 'cause she spends the whole week fussing for the people coming on Saturday.

"How many people?"

"Ask your father, they're his friends," she says. She's unpacking these boxes Dad brought, and they have dishes in them. "They'll have to do," she says when she sees them.

"Don't you have a lot of friends?" I ask.

"Yes… No… Some. These are your father's staff and *your* cousins."

"Do we have to hang around?"

She pays me no attention, like I know I said something bad, which means probably yes.

I ask Dad the same thing, "Do we have to stick around?" Even I'm getting nervous about Saturday. And Mom, she gets flying angry when she finds a sock or toy or flip-flop in her path.

"You're going to help your mother," he says.

After this she lets out a big yelp like a laugh or a squeal and doesn't say anything else.

"Or stay out of her way," he whispers.

"Dad?"

"Mmm?"

"All's the cousins ever want to do is watch TV."

"You can't expect someone to take to nature in a few hours," Dad says.

"Just thank God your father didn't ask the whole tribe," says Mom. "I guess they couldn't get out on a day pass!" Then she laughs that single chirp.

We hide in Margaret's room, combing Barbie's hair and listening to the arrivals crunch down the driveway, laugh or squeal when someone's wife or girlfriend trips or slips on the loose gravel. "City slickers," I say. We peek over the sill.

They all smell like perfume and aftershave, women with *hair doos*. Men in ironed shirts and shorts and knee socks. Women in shorts, too, and dimply legs.

Uncle René and Uncle Robert have brought our cousins. Uncle René's kids went to reformatory before and only speak French and their mom, Aunt Tati Hortense, is French, too.

They live across the river, way down the other side. Uncle Robert's girls are just freckle-faced-and-braces plain ugly.

Miss Harris, Dad's secretary, real pretty and I've seen her other summers—"*A deeevorsee*," says Mom—she always brings a different date. She looks like a movie star.

"Why's she Miss if she's divorced?" I asked Mom.

"Because she's a floozy," she whispers.

"What's a floozy?"

"Ask your father."

"Marilyn Monroe," says Mom, "was the most beautiful woman in the world." But I never saw her. To me, Miss Harris is the most beautiful woman. I never saw perfect *bottle blonde* (Mom says) hair like hers. She wears this glittery jewellery from her divorce *animoney*. Everything, says Mom, is from her settlement. Margaret says Dad likes her.

"It's called an *affair* when a man likes a woman and she's not his wife," says Margaret.

"What about her date?"

"Mom says he's a fruit," Margaret says.

"What's that?" I say.

"A grown-up sissy. Remember? Dad said."

"Is her husband from before one too?"

"No. But he thought she was a floozy."

Anyway, she has freckles from the sun and great big boobs. She brings her own diet sodas, a six-pack of Tab. She's nice. Dad likes her, too. Maybe that is an affair.

Mom fusses and gets people drinks. Serves them in the glasses we got at the gas station with the gold brims on them, her running with the drinks, licking the dribbles off her fingers.

"You kids get out here!" she shouts.

I hear that, plus my cousints' bratty voices. It's time to leave the dark and go be polite before I get heck, though "children are to be seen and not heard."

"Where's my little boyfriend?" says Miss Harris. First, all's I see is her red toenails and piggies squeezed into her golden sandals and jiggly legs into her short shorts, a shirt tied above to hold in her boobs. Next thing I know she gives me a smooching kiss and a hug. After that she lets me have one of her diet Tabs.

She changes into her tiger bathing suit with wide see-through strips like black fishing net along the sides. Still in her gold sandals she turns and her heels are wrinkly and red at the back like in school when Miss Huta takes off her shoes and we can see her heels. Miss Harris's date, the fruit, has silver hair and a suntan and really big white teeth when he smiles. Smiles more than the other men. Doesn't look like a sissy, unless they smile a whole lot.

A while passes and Margaret and me turn off the TV even though the cousints complain. If I could ditch them to see Tom I would, but he wouldn't care. He's probably doing stuff with the older guys, maybe even Jimmy now. I lead us down to the beach.

It's a swim and drinks for all the grown-ups. We walk by Miss Harris on the dock, and she's swishing the water with her legs, and we peek over her shoulder. "Two of the wonders of the world," shouts Mr. Sedaka, and all the men laugh. Miss Harris, too, but the other women *tsk tsk*.

Everyone gets in the water off O'Briens' dock. Dad bought a little Styrofoam sailboat for the party and we got the yellow paddleboard and the canoe. O'Briens got an outboard motor but Mom says that's how Mr. Whiteside met his fate, so we got a sailboat, paddleboard and canoe we barely use instead.

Dad ropes up the sailboat and plops me in, tosses me a life jacket. I turn my back to the cousins on the dock. My first time in a sailboat but I pretend it's no different than any other kind of boat. Miss Harris tries to climb in from the water and almost tips the thing and Dad helps her after that, holds her arm and finally hoists her over like when we heave Doc Smiley's dog out of the water onto the dock. She laughs and waves back at her date and he smiles and holds his drink in the air.

After ropes are tied and the sail stops swinging and Dad grabs the rudder to keep us from drifting into the shallow, and lots of laughs from the dock, we start going along good. Even Dad is surprised. Miss Harris smiles back at Dad, and he looks proud because we're going at a good splash, away from shore. Far enough out now, almost instantly, so you can see into the bay, we're way out and you can even see down and around the bend and all the faraway places look different now. The trees at our place are way smaller and some places where you could only see the roof of a place, now you can see only trees.

But now I can see thunderheads, too, waiting back up across the land and over the farmers' fields, up the river valley. The thunderheads are black at the bottom and the tops look too high and can't get any higher so they just keep spreading.

"Dad we have to go in," I say, my back to Miss Harris.

We have full sun, but now the wind whips up hard, changes direction and clips us farther away from home. Closer to the clouds now. Dad is good, for someone who never sailed. I look at Miss Harris and we smile at each other. She leans back, lets the sun shine on her neck and under her chin. She must think we do this all the time. I look at Dad to see if he notices the clouds. We're speeding now and getting farther from home, don't know what wind will take us back but it's a good wind we're riding.

Suddenly everything stops like we hit a wall so hard we tumble. Dad slides over me and Miss Harris, then me over them into the water and them in on top of me, under the water with knees and heels hitting me and then into air. I look around us at the green, bubbly water and I know where we've landed. We're in the Sargasso Sea. We're *doomed* as Mom says. Can't hardly breathe. Have to stay calm. Miss Harris is looking serious. All's we can do is stay in the water in our life jackets.

The boat pops up and sails down the river without us, the sail whipping back and forth. Miss Harris bobs in the water without a word and her hair is still perfect. Maybe she's too scared or she doesn't know the danger we're in. Dad and I start waving, but the gang on shore's way too far away. Time to time there's weeds around my legs and I go limp so as not to knot them like they said in swimming lessons. I don't know if we're in the Sargasso Sea or out. If I didn't have to stay calm for Miss Harris, I think I'd be crying right about now. But we keep yelling and waving for help until we see it. There's a boat splashing over the waves full on towards us.

It's Tom come to get us.

Sun's behind the thunderheads now and the water has turned black and the waves have turned to whitecaps, so Tom just throws us a rope and I hold on and Dad puts his arm around Miss Harris's boobs for a good grip and we get towed. But the waves make us cough so Tom stops and pulls on the rope and Dad pushes Miss Harris from behind into the back of the boat and then me up and over and finally Tom and me pull Dad in. Even now Miss Harris's hair is still perfect like a big white balloon. Dad wraps her in one of Tom's towels, arm around her to stop her shivers. I sit facing Tom. He looks at me and grins, probably because he thinks we're pretty crazy. Dad and Miss Harris ride up front.

As we get closer to home everyone's watching from the dock, saying stuff like, "I can't believe it," and, "Are you alright?" I know it was the Sargasso that saved us from going any farther and Tom saved us from the Sargasso. I don't know if he thinks I'm great 'cause I survived, or just stupid.

"Thanks Cap'n Clark," says Dad to Tom. "If you find the boat, it's yours."

How did he know we were out there?

Tom looks at me, "Joycee found the Bible." That's all he says, like it's all my fault, and away he goes.

The rain starts to hammer down a few big drops so we head upstairs to dry off. Mom is just on her way down for a swim in her new one-piece, and Uncle René is with her and they are laughing and talking. First time I've seen her laugh in a long time. They head back up with us since it's going to be a big rain. Lord knows what Joycee's mother thinks when she sees us all coming back up the hill, everyone with the giggles and the grown-ups getting drunk—even Miss Harris now.

"You should 'ave seen him," says Uncle Robert. "Monsignor Montmigny, *navigueur extraordinaire*."

"Dougaldo saved my life," says Miss Harris, quiet.

"Tomahawk did," says I.

I was thinking I'd get heck for taking off on the cousints but now it's that damn Bible I have to worry about and there's always something. Mom smiles like she's not listening. In fact she doesn't even say we could have died. Maybe it's because Miss Harris and Tom are included in the story. Maybe because Uncle René was making her laugh so much.

Dad lays big T-bones on the grill while everyone changes out of wet bathing suits and talks loud about other close calls.

"You pals with that Cap'n Clark?" asks Dad.

"Yep," I say.

"He's a good guy."

"Yep."

Finally the storm smashes right in on top of us announcing that it's here. Big chunks of hail first and then raindrops that sizzle on the grill. Everything goes dark for a bit. People laugh but Mom just stands in the kitchen with Uncle René. Then the lights come on and by the time everyone's dry and changed the sun has come out again. Steam rises off the ground and roof and it's hotter than before, but you can hear it in the hills on the other side of the river and I figure that's not the last we seen of it.

I help big dark Mr. Sedaka—we call him "Sad Sack"—unfold the picnic tables on our new veranda, end to end, and cover them with flowery plastic table cloths and all Mom's grandma's forks and knives so everyone can come onto the veranda to eat. Sad Sack says stuff like other grown-ups do, like "You're a fine young man," but some of them still think I'm a girl: "What lovely daughters," say the women after they've had some of their drinks.

Mostly the grown-ups have *discussions*, says Mom, but it sounds like fighting to me, until one of them yelps like Mom in that kind of laugh, and then they all do. By dinnertime everyone has one last drink in a glass or a beer bottle and the ice cubes are clinking. I bring Dad the wine bottles that are covered in straw and come from Italy and he starts to swear a little as he tries to pull out the corks. All the women in their colourful dresses and blouses, and the men looking sunburned

133

and in their shorts and shoes, are all there crowded onto the benches. We kids sit at the picnic table in the corner, the two girl cousints looking uglier than ever with their red hair and braces. Mom and Dad sit at the opposite ends of the big table, both laughing more than I ever seen them do.

We eat the steaks Dad barbequed, a big bowl of baked potatoes and platters of corn passed up and down the table, all dripping with butter. And for dessert, peach and blueberry pies that Mom made—her "specialty" says my dad to everyone, his face all red and smiley, and even she smiles but not at him.

After that everyone goes back in the house, watches the news on TV, and has more drinks. They pass around a two-storey box of Laura Secords that Miss Harris brought. Some men gone down by the river with a flashlight to watch the lightning on the other side. One by one the ladies use the bathroom, to "freshen up" they say. But the plywood walls don't even reach the roof because we got no ceiling and it's kinda embarrassing for them to do number two so the television is turned up louder and we know they aren't freshening up. Margaret and I and the cousints giggle but grown-ups are grown-ups. We leave them in the house.

The cousints, Margaret and me and Joycee too and her brothers make our routine that you do with company, and walk as far as Morgan's Point, opposite end of the Landing from Fitzroy's, near the empty stone house, and have to trespass waving our flashlights through the sky. I don't want to talk to Joycee and anyway she's scared I'm going to squeal about her and Tom in the bushes, and I'm scared she'll tattle about the Bible. Sometimes flashes come up behind the trees from the storm that's now long gone. Crickets sing non-stop. The woods are full of nightlife sounds, like a jungle after the rain. We walk under a no-moon starry sky. "Little diamond sparkles splashed on velvet," says Margaret.

Joycee blurts a laugh, but I don't.

"Maybe it's better we don't know the names," I say.

"Of what?"

"The stars."

"Why?"

"Then we just see them and not all that Alpha Centauri stuff, same with flowers. Trees, too. Just look with no words in your head. See what happens. Do you think God had a name for all of them?" But Joycee won't bite.

"Let's call on Tom," says Joycee.

"You call on him," I say, knowing her mom would flip if she did.

"You."

"No you," I say again.

"Dou-gal-do is jea-lous," says Joycee's brother Dan.

"I don't care who she likes," says I, and Joycee quits buggin' me. Just as well that's what they think.

We step under the barbed wire and go down the lawn, all overgrown now, to the small graveyard to sit. The boys have brought some candles to light, and they glow onto our faces if we hold them right under our chins. The candle flames reflect in Margaret's thick glasses. Joycee frowns. We all whisper. Dan, Joycee's oldest brother, looks like a pimply devil in the candlelight, starts to tell us a story we heard lots of times before around other campfires but it still scares us—the one about the people whose car stops on a deserted road and the man goes for help...

After the part where we all scream, Dan tells us to be quiet and listen. We all hear it as clear as night because none of us are breathing: a chip, chip, chipping sound. It gets louder and louder until we realize it must be one of the old gravestones being chipped at. We don't stop running until we're halfway home and we can see the lights of Tomahawk's place. I hold Margaret's chubby hand tight and practically drag her even though she can run almost as fast as me in the daytime. Her four eyes make it harder at night. Good it's night or my cousins would think I'm a sissy.

"I wouldn't have started running if all you hadn't," says Joycee.

But it was her brothers who took off first. No way I'd stay around without the older guys there.

"Let's call on Tom," she says once more.

"He's probably gone to bed," I say.

"How would *you* know?"

"Because he's *my* friend."

She runs ahead like she's not listening anymore. I bet she's hoping he'll put his arm around her. He probably did that in the bushes, maybe even kissed her pie face. I don't know why he would. I sure wouldn't. Maybe *that's* why people think I'm a sissy. Do they all think that? It doesn't matter, he saved me this afternoon.

My uncles are smoking cigars at the top of the driveway, little dots of orange glow strong and then fade and float each time they take them out of their mouths, or when they take a breath. Their voices are loud, coughing and chuckling as they wait for my cousins. Down the hill our house is dark now, only the patio lights still burning. The crickets are loud, too, around the veranda. The whole night is full, like everything is staying up late. Moths keep slamming themselves against the screen in a moth dance and click around inside the plastic patio lanterns.

There's this film of us and guests down on the dock that day, but it wasn't Mom who shot it, because she says she was up at the house. So we don't know who took it and after we saw it once we never saw it again.

THIRTEEN

"Leave your sister alone. Go find your father."

"He's hiding money."

"Then go help him."

"Not supposed to."

Screen door slams and he bangs the sand off his shoes. "The treasure hunt's done. The beach is raked. It's never looked better," he says. "You kids stay away from there until it's time."

"We're going in the boat race."

"Over my dead body," says Mom.

"It's O'Briens' boat."

"Wear a life jacket," she says. "Mr. Whiteside, he even wore…"

Then Margaret and me look at each other and interrupt her: "*That's how Mr. Whiteside died. The boat kept going around and around...*"

But Mom says nothing back.

"Dougaldo wants to cheat," says Margaret.

"I don't want to, but I could if I wanted to. That's all. All the boats have different horsepower."

"There'll be no cheating," says Mom.

"Someone has to cheat to win."

"In theory," says Dad.

No sign of Tomahawk for some days, give him a rest from me, maybe make him want to see me more, like Mom should do with Dad.

"You going to race with Tom?" says Margaret.

"Not today."

"But you're pals."

"Do you think?"

"You going to race with me and Joycee?" asks Margaret.

"Yep."

"Then what if Joycee says I can't come?"

"Then I won't go either," I say.

Sometimes I like being nice to Margaret.

Joycee's waiting on the dock, her arms folded, tapping her foot.

"Dad says we can't cheat," says Margaret.

"Can't cheat in a five horsepower anyway," I say. "Not like Tom's nine." Joycee doesn't say anything. I got her over a barrel since I saw her in the bushes.

We pull up to the Clarks'. All the boats bobbing like bark in a stream, different shapes and sizes. Folks on shore shouting out to the boats. Even swim instructor Jimmy has his speedboat there. He has the 120 on it that roars noise into everyone's place, no escaping it. Mapothers' houseboat is in, too, usually just sits in the river all summer, and two different forties on two different boats, one a Johnson and one a Merc. I like the tall black Merc but Tom says they run shitty.

Then Tom comes out of the bunkhouse and races down the hill, and he's got Jerry Mapother, who only comes up on weekends, following him. They jump in his nine just in time. I look at Joycee and she asks what I'm looking at: "Why does Tom want to play with that runt Mapother, anyway?"

We sit Margaret in the front this year so everyone will think we can't go as fast as we want to because she's too chubby. Tom pulls up, and Joycee just keeps staring ahead, but just as I go to nod hello, fat Mr. Mapother, Jerry's Grampa, snaps two big pieces of two by four and we're off. Tom shoots ahead and Jimmy's boat roars and stands up like high-ho silver before he takes off with a twenty-foot rooster tail, and all the other boats zip ahead of ours, which means, since start and finish are the same line, we're closer to the finish line than any of them. Joycee drives and won't look at me, just looks ahead to Tom's boat like she wants to catch it.

"Slow down!" I shout. "We have to go out slow before we turn. Okay—flag's down. Turn, turn! Speed up!"

She turns hard and Margaret switches to the middle with me, so we can come back faster. Even so we hear Jimmy's boat roar behind. And then Tomahawk and Jerry slip by, which means they all probably cheated.

"It's all your fault!" Joycee shouts at me. "You and your stupid sister."

"You didn't go slow enough out!" I shout.

Me and Margaret just look at each other like Joycee's crazy.

"Stupid idea, cheating," I say, knowing it'll bug the 'vangelis part of her.

Next is swimming. We all float beside Mapothers' raft waiting for the start. Blocks snap. Pull the water. Don't look down. Breathe at the bleach bottles. Turn. Pull harder. White water. Bubbles. All's I see is feet in front of me, lots of them. Margaret screaming now. I see her jumping and her hands clapping. Am I winning? I take a breath. But they're all at the end before me. Every single one of them.

The grown-ups from all around start to show up. Then there's all the other races up on the beach—wheelbarrow, three-legged...

"Why don't you partner with Joycee?" says Tom.

"She's *your* girlfriend," I say. "Besides Margaret's my partner."

"You and the girls."

"You and Joycee."

Tom's with Jerry still. Even though Jerry's short and looks like a chipmunk, he's so strong he holds Tom up by the ankles at the starting line. Tom's feet in his face. Maybe I push Margaret a bit too fast because her arms cave in and I go flying over her and grind her head into the sand, like I squashed her. She's okay, alive anyway, but crying. I pull her off the beach and we limp over to Mom, sitting on a fold-out chair.

"What did you expect?" Mom looks around and everyone looks away, laughs like it's only a kid that's crying, not realizing she was nearly killed. "You kids shush." Tomahawk doesn't look our way.

The water balloon toss comes along for the older ones, except not my parents. With Mom's bigness, like Dad said, I figure she thinks people laugh at her jugs. But all the ladies' boobs bounce as if the balloons are down their shirts. They try to keep everything tucked in but that's usually how they miss and get soaked. There's Ginny, Jackie and Debbie, sisters, married but looking young. They like to flirt with me. They're all smiles and laughs and bouncy even when they get soaked, like girls in toothpaste commercials. But they are pretty.

The men wear shorts and some of them even have strong legs but when they take their shirts off you can tell they go to the office the rest of the year with funny tans around their necks and bulgy middles. Tomahawk's dad doesn't look like a dad 'cause of his police muscles all over him.

Old man Mapother—Jerry's Grampa—he's in charge of opening pop for us. Jerry's dad is dead but his mom, Gramp, Gran are still alive. Cream soda is good for spraying all over them others. It's the most pressurized. When the sand sticks to it and it sticks to us it makes us look like "filthy Injuns," says Mom, loud enough for Tomahawk to hear. Maybe even his dad can hear, too. Tom and his dad are sitting with Doc Smiley and Doc's wife the nurse, and the monkey brats of course. I don't go near them, especially after the Baby Huey thing, and what I heard of the Tom's dad and Nurse Smiley thing. But more because I know they don't like my mom and all's she can do is talk behind their backs anyway.

Don't see Tom's mom.

We take our pop and towels up the steps to Mapothers' place, a huge grassy lawn like houses in the city have. Stuff's all new—swings, chairs, loungers, barbeque, patio lights and wire drink holders—even though they only come on weekends. Some women rush home to get changed out of wet clothes but the rest of us kids stay dirty, and sticky too, if you got shot with soda.

Jerry's mom makes the best baked beans, sweet and crusty. But Mom says she doesn't look like she ever pulled so much as a crumb out of the oven. She's not like the other moms. Never looks like it's a hot day. Most ladies are in shorts and slacks but she's in a frilly dress, and her shiny red hair curls at her shoulders like spools of copper trolling wire. She talks to Dad.

143

"Looks like she's off to a wedding," says Mom to Mrs. O'Brien. "The merry widow."

And there's tables full of wieners, hamburgs, potato salad and salad of every colour with marshmallows and jelly that'll make you sick, 'specially after cream soda, but for dessert there's chocolate cake, brown sugar squares and buckets of Smarties. Dad and Jerry Mapother's mom keep laughing quietly through trophy time.

"Dougaldo Montmigny, swimming, nine-to-twelve-year-olds." I can't move, hearing my name out loud like that. I'm stuck behind the chairs and then someone pushes me and they're laughing and shouting. Even though I was last, I'm the only one in my age group. That's why. They're all older. Margaret claps but Mom and Mrs. O'Brien keep busy, whispering.

There's swimming lesson stuff, and the whole group of us gets our Senior Red Cross, even me. Jimmy shakes our hands, smiling, too, 'cause he's not near the water to drown us.

"Jimmy's got a hairy rat," Tomahawk whispers.

"What?"

"Red hair, too."

I sit with the moms and look over at Tom. When did he see Jimmy's rat? Soon it's time to go and moms pack and divvy up food and others pack up chairs and blankets and head home to put on bug spray for the baseball game. Tom is still standing by Jerry and they wrestle a bit. Nothing I know how to do. I bruise when I get punched in the shoulder. I walk to the ball diamond with Margaret and Joycee. Mom and Dad walk ahead with Joycee's folks. I run up behind to put Mom's and Dad's hands together. Dad gives me a shove.

"Now why'd you do that?" says Mom. I think she's scolding Dad until I see she's talking to me.

"Sorry," I say.

Dad doesn't try to hold her hand anyway.

The game is always Baird's Landing against Billings' Bay at the diamond across from Madeline's. Madeline has the okay, from Tom's dad, to sell beer for the game. I don't see Tomahawk or Jerry Mapother anywhere at all. Maybe they're off smoking.

Grown-ups play baseball bad as they do the water balloons. And if Big Red could throw the ball as far as the bat she'd be in the Olympics. She almost nails my shins. Not everyone plays, including mine and Joycee's parents, but everyone drinks beer, talks till it's dark.

Tom and Jerry don't even come back after dark and Margaret and I walk alone. Folks around us, I stare up to the sky and watch for shooting stars to make a wish that Tom and me will be brothers…

"She's a floozy," I hear Mom say from out of the dark.

"Maybe so, but that was her date," says Dad.

"Are they talking about Jerry's mom?" I whisper.

"Oh everyone knows he's a fruit. You said so yourself. You called him a *maudite-Crees* sissy. Those were your words."

"Must be Miss Harris," says Margaret.

145

"He's her latest," Dad says.

"Mom gets jealous when Dad talks to ladies," Margaret says.

"Don't lie to me," Mom whisper-talks. "I know exactly what's going on between you and her."

Then Ginny, Jackie and Debbie, the married sisters, run up to me, put their arms on my shoulders and play with my hair, giggle and shove me.

"Look at Dougaldo," says Dad loud. "He's already a ladies' man."

"Saints preserve us," says Mom.

Others around us laugh in the dark.

There's this black-and-white picture pinned to the wall in my parents' bedroom. Mom and Dad are way out on the sandbar, out at the island, far apart but running, arms reaching towards each other. Looks like they're running on the water. Like in a Hollywood movie. All's you can see is Mom way far away and Dad's backside closer to the camera. Maybe Uncle René took the picture.

FOURTEEN

"They only come 'cause the town bores them," I say.

"You hold your tongue," Mom says, so I do.

"Get your filthy hands out of your mouth! You'll choke on the germs."

"I thought we didn't have to have them again after he came and his mom brought that cake. Last time all's we did was crash his rocket, eat hot dogs, watch TV and then they went home. You even said you were killing yourself to see them go."

"I did not."

"Anyways they went away somewhere for the summer."

"They're back," says Mom. "I already talked to his mother."

"Can he bring his tent?"

"Does he have a tent?"

"I wish I did."

"If it will shut you up."

I run to Tomahawk's and ask him, "Do you want to have a sleepover?"

"In the bunkhouse?"

"No. My place."

"What about your mom?"

"In a tent."

"You have a tent?"

"Sort of."

"Two of us?"

"Almost. It's only Geoff, you and me—Jerry can't come. No room."

"Jerry's gone back to the city."

So after Geoff and me have weenies at the beach, Tom shows up and he doesn't talk or anything. He has his sleeping bag. "Skinny-dip?"

And this is good 'cause for a sec Geoff was looking like, *What's Tom doing here?* We get into our birthday suits. Tom waves his dink in the air. But Geoff's head is in the clouds. Tom's rat is hairiest.

It's too dark now for nosy Mrs. O'Brien. Folks think we're having a bonfire, but all we do is light the rubbing alcohol that Geoff had in a jar, and then throw branches on it. I make sure Margaret isn't allowed to bug us. I just holler "Mom!" and then she calls Margaret. Margaret doesn't care. She's only jealous of me when I'm with Joycee, and I hate Joycee anyway.

"I'm Neptune," says Geoff. But it's Tom who gets wrestley, and tries to drown Geoff. We grab each other, pretending we can't see. We do shoulder rides. I don't think they care but I like it when my dink is touching the back of someone's neck before they pitch me in.

In the tent we're still bare-skinned and getting the sleeping bags spread. Geoff reads his comics with a flashlight, peels the edges of the parts he's read, chews them, and then swallows it! The Cheezies make a mess on our fingers and blankets. Geoff ignores us. I don't care. Mom invited him. He puts on his transistor radio like that's more important, and it is, because we can hear a station all the way from Syracuse, New York, coming in and out.

"It's because we're on the river," says Geoff, and then he peels more edge off his comic and eats it. We try to wrestle him to get him to fight back, but he swats us like flies with his comic book.

I pick up one of the comics and flip through, look for Bazooka Joe prizes with Tom at my shoulder. He squats, knees to his chest, and his rough feet just touch mine, and I breathe fast from the chill I get. He leans close. His skin so much darker and dark hair on his legs never gets light from the sun. His back widens when he bends over the comics. I feel good 'cause it must be going to happen to me, too. I want to be strong like him. I don't want to be Mr. Skin and Bones. He's so close. I don't want to be afraid. I just want to touch him.

149

We bed down onto our backs, tired, and listen to this song they play lots since the beginning of summer called "Strangers in the Night" (Mom loves it and Dad says it's the worst song he ever heard). We're wailing and waving our hands to the top of the tent like we're conducting a choir, and change the words to "Do be do be do, *with seven children*," until we're all out of breath.

"Your mom going to die?" I say.

"Maybe. Nurse Smiley says no, if Mom keeps taking her medicine."

"Does she?"

"She says the medicine is killing her."

"What do you do when you take care of her?"

"I read to her."

"Movie mags?"

"No, not movie mags. Bible mostly. Makes her calm."

"Bible? Why didn't you tell me?"

"You never asked."

"I just thought Injuns…"

"You think too much about Injuns…"

"But Thierry on TV…"

"Forget Thierry. It's all made up."

"You have a Bible—you 'vangelis?"

"I just read her the Bible is all."

"Dad has a religion. Catholic. Says he's fed up with goddamn Catholics. But I'm sort of nothing, 'cause Mom's a pedestrian or prebsyterranean or whatever. Say my prayers though."

"Me too."

"When did you see Jimmy's rat?" I say.

"Out in the boat."

"He showed it to you?"

"Wanted to see mine too but wouldn't let him."

"Why not?"

"He wanted to talk about growing-up stuff."

"Like what?"

"Touching it. It tickles."

"You do that?" I say.

"You?"

"I don't know. Did you see Jerry's?"

"In the bunkhouse, yep."

"Touch it?"

"Yep."

"Hairy?"

"Not yet."

"Do they all get hairy?"

"All of them. Even yours."

I hear Geoff wheezing to sleep, then Tom, too. Beside me at last.

FIFTEEN

Geoff and me wake up but no Tom, he's gone. His sleeping bag is gone, too, like he was never here. I guess he knows to stay away in daylight. Mrs. O'Brien and my mom are nothing but trouble. I feel good he was here. He talked to me, too. Said I'd even have hair down there. That kind of stuff. Like maybe brothers talk about.

Soon Geoff goes back to the harbour, so I pretend I'm kinda sad but want to go and find Tom once Geoff's gone for good. I want to talk more like we did last night and read comics, too, with him beside me. I know we can do that again.

"Joycee's mom says she heard everything that went on in that tent," says Mom. "Says the half-breed spent the night."

"Didn't do anything, and his name is Tom."

"Tomfoolery! The three of you could have suffocated in there, or drowned if they'd opened the dam. Anyway we're taking you to camp. You better start thinking about what you're going to take because we leave this afternoon."

I won't make it over to Tom's and all I wanted was to read comics, be by him for a little longer. Now he'll forget the fun we had, and then he'll think I don't care about him and that I'd rather take off to camp. Then he won't care at all. No more trips out to Sargasso Sea. No chance of another sleepover, ever. No feet touching by accident or on purpose.

There I am standing beside a green duffle bag almost big as me, holding a paddle, the first time I went to camp. Goofy smile on my face, not knowing what camp is and Margaret skipping happy all around me like it's in slow motion. And after, she was upset. She wanted to go, too.

Now Joycee's at the door.

"Here." She holds out her hand with a folded paper in it. "Father always says this to my brothers when they fight. If you can get a Bible you'll be able to find it in it, then you can make blood brothers."

"Why?"

"Camp will make you a good Christian. Mother says so."

"Christians don't make blood brothers, only Injuns."

"Just take it."

I know it's because she's happy to have Tom all to herself for the next two weeks and I hate her.

It takes us all afternoon to get to Camp Gesthemane. The licence plates are coloured and there are lots of pretend places on the way: Santa's Village and Land of Make Believe. Margaret wants to go to Santa's.

But driving in, this camp is like a big hotel–motel for kids. Tall trees everywhere, no undergrowth at all, just pine needles on the ground. And it doesn't smell like our pines, in fact it barely smells at all. Dad coughs a bit and then Mom even has some tears.

"Don't forget to take your pill," says Mom, "or you'll be stuck in a wet sleeping bag. It's not like home. I can't change your sheets." I don't know where Michigan is but it's where they're going to see Mom's cousins. Only two weeks is all I can think. Time will go faster if I count each day.

A lady comes to us right off the bat, takes Margaret away. Her looking back, over her shoulder, starting to cry, and my heart choking me. Then a big girl with a wide bum, wider than Big Red's, grabs my hand. Pulls me. We go past pioneer log buildings, a fenced-in place where there are all these horses, and then a place where kids are lying on their stomachs shooting rifles at little squares of paper hanging on a clothesline far away. Horses don't look like they care. In the movies it always bugs them. It would bug me if I was a horse. Dad says guns are for cowards—gives the shooter an unfair advantage. He knows these kinds of things. There's other people shooting bows 'n arrows at bull's eyes. And then older kids standing shooting pistols at pictures of birds and bears.

Trees keep going everywhere in every direction, and a big mountain behind. Opposite way is a lake, not as big as the river. Bleach bottles in it so you don't go out past over your head. Sailboats. Farther along to the left is a wood barn covered by the biggest tent I ever saw, like a movie theatre, but you can't have movies at camp, 'specially 'vangelis camps.

"That's where *bahbuhl* rallies are," says this big girl who's holding my hand.

"Oh," says I. But I don't know what one of them is.

"Every night, at seven o'clock."

"Like games? Relays?" I say.

She whistles out her nose.

After that we come to a long line of log cabins.

"You're in Mark."

"Oh."

"As in Mark, Luke and John."

"What's that?"

"As in, 'Hold the horse and I get on?'"

"Oh yeah," I say.

"The *decahples*? The *uh-postles*? *Sayunts*?"

"No numbers only names?"

"Books of the Bible!"

"Isn't there just one book?" I say.

She nose-whistles again.

Mark was empty but it looked like people lived there and there were socks and sleeping bags all messed together with shoes.

"They're on their way back from pistol practice."

"Where's the 'firmery?"

"The…" she clears her throat, kinda fakey high, "*in…*" she stops a second, "*…firmary?*"

"Yeah that's where I'm supposed to take my pill." I'm not going to tell her why.

She talks slow. "Go straight through those trees and you'll come to a small *guh-rey bayuilding.*" She points to where some kids are coming down the road. I think they're heading for here. As they get closer I see their dirty faces and dirt-dried snot under their noses. Camp kids are never clean. Now I have to meet them.

"Here are your *compaynyuns,*" she calls them.

They been here already for two weeks at least or even more, so I'm a real stranger. She introduces me to Jesse, our counsellor. He looks kind of like a boy only way bigger. He has whiskers, a suntan, and thick legs. He's holding a stick with a little piece of leather on it that he slaps on his hand. And he twitches his head to keep the hair out of his eyes. Like he was in the *Teen Beat* magazine I seen at Madeline's.

"Douglas?"

"Hi." I won't tell him Dougaldo. "Doug."

"*Hello* to your elders."

That's when the lady turns and goes, not even goodbye.

"Hello," I say.

He switches the stick and holds his hand out. I shake it. It's big, so I know he's a real grown-up. Thicker than swim instructor Jimmy's. "You want lunch?"

"Sure."

"Then no back talk."

"I didn't back talk."

"No back talk, sissy."

Two other boys come up, twins, everyone calling them Fric and Frac but I bet that's not their real names. Look like kids I seen from other summers, bean-shaves and peeling skin on their cheeks. Mostly frowns, though. All different. Even a Negro guy, Franklin, but light brown skin. No surprise 'cause I seen others here, just more of them. Like the one in my school, Deborah. She teaches us songs like, "Dem Bones." Sounding African. But this guy don't talk like Deborah, he says words like *ekscape* and *ekspecially* and *nuffin'* and *s'posad be*. Everyone knows it's *asposed to be*.

And they aren't too nice to Franklin anyhow. They talk kind of rough to him and tell him to shut up but maybe it's just joking around. But I think we better be nice to him at a 'vangelis camp. Besides they're just the same as us but with tans, mostly. And I'm sure O'Briens try to be nice for God.

"You from *Keeyanuhduh*? They got kings and queens up there."

"Only one."

"Kings and queers!"

"Eh?"

157

"Don't backtalk."

"Eh?" I say.

"B? C? D? E?"

"You're making fun of me?" I think they don't like different here too much.

"Hey Frenchie, where ya from? No back talk, Frenchie, or Jesse'll swat you wid his riding crop."

In the dining hall I can't talk. Like all the other years, I look at the ceiling and swallow a lot. I know if I don't swallow the tears won't go down my throat. They'll come out my eyes and everyone will notice and then they'll laugh. But I think everyone knows what's the matter but no one says anything. So I look at the rafters. Every dining hall has rafters.

"*Keeyanuhduh*," they say. "They got igloos up there and Ekskimos too."

Only thirteen days to go, I think to myself.

At night I dream about the Sargasso Sea, except it's clear and there's no weeds, just bright beams of sun travelling down into the deep. I can see the golden bottom and it doesn't frighten me. Like pictures I seen of the Grand Canyon. I see big cliffs of rock under the water reflecting streams of the sun's rays up like orange and yellow. No people, no Margaret, kids or fish. Not even Tom. Maybe not even me. It doesn't scare me. It's just peace and quiet, that's all.

And I shouldn't dream this dream, because anytime I dream about water it means my bed is going to be wet and I even know it in the dream. Looks like I'll be sleeping in a wet sleeping bag for a few nights.

"Each day you're going to have target practice, riflery, archery, horseback riding, sailing, canoe and swim lessons," says Jesse. He talks slow like them others, too, like he has to think about what he wants to say all the time before each word.

"Hey Frenchie, get in the water," says Jesse.

I know better. Too many kids makin' this giant whirlpool and lifeguards have to keep pulling half-drowned kids out of the undertow before they disappear under the floating dock. They don't get it.

"Frenchie!"

"Too dangerous," I shout back at him.

Jesse's bunk is right under mine but sticking out like a T-shape, and in the morning of eleven-more-days-to-go I wake up on the floor under his bunk. It doesn't hurt but I don't know how I got there unless someone put me there. They picked on Franklin when I got here, and this other guy, Boston Justin, 'cause he talks funny, but I'm Frenchie and a late one so it's me who gets picked on by the guys who say they're my friends.

"I can't change being from Canada," I say.

"Think you're better than us?" says a pudgy guy they call Pudgy. I don't say anything and that makes him madder.

Another guy, Pike, dirty and always picking his nose, wipes it on his shirt, says stupid stuff.

"It's not *couple this* and *couple that*," I explain to him.

"Maybe not in Canada."

"And not *fifteen of*, whatever that means. All's you have to do is tell the time."

They pin me on Jesse's bed. Lift up my shirt. Tickle me too much, and slap my belly till I cry. They won't stop. I'm going to wet my pants but even that doesn't happen only because there's no pee in me.

"Fairy, fairy, Frenchie," they all start calling me while they're slapping my stomach. "God don't like fairies. Fairies is just dirty old fruits." I lie on my bunk, back to them. Maybe that's what Tomahawk meant when he called me momma's boy. Maybe I do like him like a girl.

Except for me, everyone has a Bible, and all I have is a souvenir prayer book, so I can look for *saw-ums* whenever I want 'cept I can't find it. And for Bible rally we go to the theatre. Jesse calls it the Holy-wood Bowel. I don't get it. So a guy called Uncle Jack, whose camp this whole place is, he starts preachin'. He makes me think of the television guys and a woman called Kathryn Kuhlman. I love her. She talks to you like she can see you sitting there outside your TV set, and so I sit real close to the TV so maybe she can see me. Don't know what she talks about but sometimes she cries and makes me cry, too.

So Uncle Jack shouts to us, "Come down and accept *Jaysus* into your heart!" The guys whisper and shove me so I walk down and kneel on the floor in front of everyone, and he says some things and then *Jaysus* is in my heart after that. My heart still feels the same, though. Just sad mostly. No point that I'm not with Tom. I look around after accepting *Jaysus* and I can't move. The bowel looks like a huge upside-down canoe, rafters like ribs. I see my group smilin' at me. Everyone sings "I Know Where I'm Going." Back at my seat the guys have ripped all the pages out of my souvenir prayer book.

On Sunday after church or worship or whatever they call it, and after we've sang "Rise and Shine and Give God the Glory" about a thousand times, I go to look for Margaret. We're allowed to see each other once and that's on Sunday. Anyone who has a sister gets to see them. They bring them over in the war canoe. But I can't find the canoe or any people until I see Margaret on the porch of the dining hall wiping her eyes. Her little yellow summer dress Mom likes her to wear is brown now, and she doesn't notice me till I'm close.

"I thought you forgot," she says.

Her fingernails are all dirty and her eyes red from crying. Her whole face is puffy like when Joycee and I tease her and she cries. Looks like she tried to cut her own bangs, too. I start to cry. I hug her real hard. Don't want her to know I'm crying.

"Did you cut your hair?"

"Yep."

"It looks real nice."

We have lunch with my cabin guys in the dining hall and they giggle. Me and Margaret just look at each other and eat but she looks all the while like she's going to start crying again, like when you got food in your cheeks and can't swallow it, and now I can feel something in my heart and it still isn't *Jaysus*, it just feels like a big crack down the middle 'cause I hate to see her have to be all alone and unhappy.

There is a song-and-dance show after lunch put on by the girl counsellors and that makes us less sad. But even when Margaret's smiling when I'm looking at her and she doesn't know, it hurts in my heart. After that, I take her outside to say bye and thank *Jaysus* that all the brats from my cabin have gone somewhere. She starts to cry.

"Only one more week," I say, but then I start to cry. And a big canoe comes and takes all the sisters away like little white Injun squaws going back to the far shore, the girls' camp. Now I just count the seconds till it's all over and they come and get us and take us home.

One of the guys, Mac Osler—Hoser they call him—real gangly and his eyes are all baggy and tired most of the time, comes to me in the evening. "Why djoo have to go to da 'firmary?"

I don't talk.

"You wetcher bed?"

He grins 'cause he figured it out. I hope he can't smell it.

"Don't tell them, *please*."

"'S'okay," he says. He grins again. Friendly.

He seems nice. "You ever do blood brothers?"

"Nope. Don't want to."

162

"Why not?"

"I got enough brothers. Plus you got to kiss."

I go for my green pills at the 'firmary. No one said anything about a kiss. Don't know if Tom would want to kiss me. I could have kissed Tom in his sleep. But it would make me laugh. It's not so bad walking along the lighted cabins thinking about that, until I'm walking through a clearing, then the trees. It's dark. I say that thing I heard at the Bible rally and Kathryn Kuhlman says sometimes too, "Yay though I walk through the valley of the shadow of death." But the trees are mean and there's no stars so I think of Tom with me and then I run till I see the lights of the 'firmary.

"You keep forgetting to come," says the nurse, "unless there's been divine intervention and you're cured. Lord love a duck!" She doesn't look like a nurse, not with those white things they wear and stockings and all. She looks more like a grown-up in kids' clothes. I don't want to talk about the wet sleeping bag. And the pills are green with a little blue stamp on them and if you keep it in your mouth long enough before you swallow you can taste a taste like if you put your finger in your ear and then taste it, or lick the screen door. I take it and say thank you to be polite, and then run all the way back to the cabin.

Maybe it's fairies that wet their beds. Maybe it's these pills I take that make you not a fairy. Is Tomahawk in his bunkhouse? Is Jerry Mapother there? Are blood brothers fairies? Homos? Do they take lots of showers?

On our two-day canoe trip, I ride in Jesse's canoe. If you stick close to him he's not as mean. He wears a shirt on his head like a India Injun. Behind him I stare at his feet bottoms. Toes, even and soft, like pads on a dog's or cat's feet. They remind me of Tom's.

At night we set up camp on an island. Everything is wet from rain last night. Boston Justin, always a curl in his forehead, and always combed, too, starts to cry 'cause his sweater got wet that day with all his stuff. When he talks he sounds like he got marbles balancing on his tongue. But that's not the worst. What really makes him cry is when he puts his sweater over a branch by the fire to dry and burns half his sweater away. So he's crying and saying his parents will be *furious*.

"Quit whining," shouts Hoser, even though I know for a fact he pees his bed, too.

They all start to yell at Justin and then someone says I should do something. "Show us you aren't a homo." Then everyone says it, so I go over to Justin.

"Quit crying!" I shout. Then they shout at me and the louder they shout, the louder I shout. And the more of a baby Justin is. His curl still stuck on his forehead.

I don't know where it's coming from but I'm yelling. The others sit in a circle. Maybe now they're afraid of me. I want to yell at all of them. Scare all of them. Make them know I'm no fairy. If I don't shout down Boston Justin then it's me next.

"Quit crying!" I shout again. And he wails. Even I don't cry like that.

I go to whack him. I won't punch, don't know how anyway and that might really hurt. So I slap his hands away from his face. He keeps covering his face and the more he does the more I keep swatting them, like he's a punching doll. But I don't think I'm hurting him. And he knows that, too. But it sounds bad. Other guys don't say anything.

"Quit whining!" is what I shout, and then I shout "*Maudite Cureestu!*" All the guys laugh. Justin gets up off the ground and we start chasing him, tear branches off trees and he runs like a scared rabbit, always checking behind with his wild eyes. He flies up and down over the logs, under branches snapping through the forest. Sycamore's most painful. Then we lose him. All of us cut by the branches and me not too proud of what I did. Not like a fairy, though.

I think of dead Chester McBride in the woods. I always knew it was all of our faults and all we did was run through the woods, never even laid a finger on him. Now I think we're doing the same thing, maybe worse. "We have to wait for him," I say, which sounds like I want to wait and beat the shit out of him. I don't mean it to, but I guess the guys think I'm a real fighter.

"He gonna be back," says Mac Osler. And then the guys take off towards the light by the tents. I wander around in the dark bashing my toes on stumps and rocks, then fall on Boston Justin near the tent. He's crouched by a tree—shivering.

"Please leave me alone."

"I'm sorry."

165

"Don't hurt me."

"I said I'm sorry. I'm really, really sorry."

"I forgive you," he says.

"You ever do the blood brother thing?"

"No."

"Come back," says I.

"Don't worry about me."

"You have to come now."

"I'll come, I'm okay. I know you didn't mean it, you're a gentleman, that's what my father would say, a gentleman…"

"Let me hold onto you."

"I'm alright."

"You're shivering. I'll hold you."

"You're so warm."

"Please don't stay out here."

"I'll be there soon," he says. I hear the voices off in the distance. Justin is trembling now, like a scared mouse or a dying pup. "They'll call us fairies," he whispers. "Are you?"

"I don't think so." And now dead Chester scares me less. I could have been there to save him even though Mom says he'd already made up his mind. I think of those guys, my friends, back at school and of sitting by the warm wall on Sports Day. I think of Tom and how where he is must be warm and dry—maybe reading to his mom or in the bunkhouse with that Jerry. Maybe I should have taken one of those guns at the riflery range and shot them guys and me and Margaret make a run for those big tree branch gates. Hide in Santa's Village until someone comes to rescue us.

In the morning, Justin and me are still shivering by the same tree trunk, beside his wet clothes. Everything on me is achy and cold, and both of us have chattering teeth. I wrap Justin in blankets. Jesse doesn't ask any questions. He can go to hell. And everyone including Jesse just keeps real quiet.

Back at camp, it's our last day and night and the bell rings to get everyone to come to where we had our Bible rallies.

"You're here in the name of *Jaysus* Christ," says Uncle Jack, but we know it's more for the party or to make us feel good so we won't tell our parents how much we hated camp. There's baskets of Cheezies, potato chips and we have hot dogs, too, not like a weenie roast but more like from Royal Burger or a restaurant or something, even wrapped in foil. But no Coke—only Kool-Aid and some other drink I never seen, not even at Madeline's. Dr. Peppler?

Everyone's chattery, people getting awards. Then they call my name and give me this little dark carved frowny face for being "congeniality," whatever that means. I know it's a good thing I stayed in the woods with Justin, and maybe that's why they gave me this. Anyways it has a shoelace to tie it around my neck. Looks like it was carved by a witch doctor.

In the morning I keep looking at my prize, and the guys tell me they're going to take away the homo thing if I don't stop looking at it and start cleaning up the cabin. A big inboard,

167

looking like a bus on the water, and not the canoe brings the girls over to our camp this time, and I smile when I finally see Margaret and she's smiling because it really means we're going home, and she and me go sit where we were left in the first place and wait like we're friends now, too.

"He wants to say goodbye," she says.

I look around and there's a station wagon slowly coming by. Hand reaching out the back window. It's Boston Justin looking as cleaned and scrubbed as I seen him all week, even with a smile on his face. No tear streaks.

"We weren't really friends."

"Go say goodbye."

I go up to the car to shake his hand.

"Best of luck," he says, in his marble-mouth way. "We were friends," he says to his parents, like he's real proud and then the car drives away.

"Nobody really liked him," I said to Margaret. "Guess I feel sorry for him." Maybe something like that happened in her cabin and I guess I want someone to tell me I'm not a big turd.

We wait in this dusty parking lot all afternoon until even after the sun has gone behind the trees and Margaret has finished her comics and eaten all her black balls. She was saving them to take back home or at least have in the car, 'cause you can't buy them in Canada. "Shadows are growing," she says. Then the car spins into the parking lot, raising dust and gravel, too. Mom is just staring straight ahead. Maybe Dad got lost.

I'm happier than them because we get to stay in a motel tonight, and there will be wrapped soap and matches and maybe even free fly swatters at the good ones, and we still have some weeks till school.

"Have you and Dad accepted *Jaysus* into your hearts yet?" I say.

"Jesus Murphy!" says Mom to Margaret. "Who cut your hair?"

And even though me and Margaret usually share a bed at motels, this time Dad sleeps with me and Mom with Margaret, and Mom and Dad don't really talk too much like as if they aren't even happy to see us or anything. Maybe they heard I'm a fairy from someone. It doesn't matter now because the motel bed is big and dry.

The next day we drive through this town. Pretty houses with porches, big trees and lawns all cut, flowers and flags everywhere. A rushing river on the other side of the road, and a park, too.

"Did you take pictures and movies in Michigan?" But Mom pretends she doesn't hear me.

"Small-town USA," she says. First thing she says since they picked us up. "Them and their silly flags."

"There was a flood here years ago," says Dad.

"A flood?"

"A spring flood," says Dad. "We did a story on it."

"See that house?" And Dad points to a big porched house all blue and white.

"Yeah."

"Two lovers stood on the roof of their car and as the water..."

"Oh you're not going to tell that *silly* story," says Mom. "You don't even know if that's the house."

"Tell us, tell us," me and Margaret say, even bouncing on the seat.

But Mom butts in fast and talks real quickly, "...and they stood there holding hands and the water came up and washed them away and that was the end of them. Forever and ever, amen."

"They died," I say to Margaret.

"I guess so," says Dad.

"Maybe they got washed away to an island," says Margaret and she presses her forehead on the window.

As we go by where maybe they lived, I can see it happening. Dad said the man could have saved himself but not both of them so he decided to die with her. When he says this, Mom lets out one of those laughs like when someone says something real stupid—too stupid to say it's stupid.

"Why didn't they swim?" I say.

"The water's like a strong wind, only thicker. It just pulls you down," Dad says.

"Like at camp—it was pulling those kids under," I say.

170

"Don't fill their heads with this nonsense," huffs Mom. We're quiet and Margaret is even snoring for a while. I think of that dream that made me pee. Dad speeds us past Santa's and the Land of Make Believe and even Frontier Town, like he's afraid I'll notice, I bet. It's been maybe an hour gone by but I have to say something important before we get to the border: "Mom? Dad? Did you accept *Jaysus* into your hearts?"

"*Christ!* Presbyterians were already born like that," Mom shouts.

"Like what?" I say. I know it bugs her.

"Only Catholics will see the pearly gates," Dad says.

"Don't fill their heads with this nonsense." Mom huffs now.

Second time she's talked since we left. Even so, she seems happier now we're going back to Canada.

Out of the town and back on the big highway Americans have—they call it a turnpike—and the traffic gets slow and we drive past a burning car and a family of Negroes standing outside of it crying and the big mom holding a little baby in her arms. All's I want is to go back to Canada where we don't have turnpikes and hotel-motels or even floods except in the spring in the bay—but that always happens, and no one's there to drown.

SIXTEEN

With my eyes closed and my head on the car seat I follow in
my mind where I think we are until we turn onto the gravel—
then I know for sure. Mom is snoring, her head bobbing. Dad's
leaning over the steering wheel. Leaning north, like we always
say, because that's what's in front of us. There's a green glow
and shadow on the inside of the car from the dials on the
dashboard. All's quiet except for the roar on the gravel. I get
up from lying on the seat just as we go past Tomahawk's. The
lights are off there.

That night the veranda's cold, colder than two weeks ago,
but when I wake up the sun's warm on my face and I smell
the sheets to make me know I'm really home and not just
dreaming. I try not to remember where I was for two weeks.

Summer will be over even if I don't do blood brothers,
so I put my stuff in my pockets and take what's left of the

Laura Secords Miss Harris brought—the ones people squeeze but don't want to eat.

.If you walk from our dock along the beach as far as Tom's, along the flat rock, you pass a huge, round boulder sitting up on the rocky shelf, all crossed with white lines. It isn't like any of the other rocks on the shore or in the river 'cause it's a meteor. There isn't any other explanation—it came from outer space. It's where we all used to meet in other summers, and past there and up the hill from that I can just see Tomahawk's bunkhouse.

"Tom, you in there?"

Tom comes to the door, eyes under his bangs like he doesn't give a hoot, looking at a place past me.

"What're you doing?" I say. He doesn't answer or anything. Just opens the door. I go in. We sit on the bunk. Now he's got an old TV in there. It's not on but he stares at it, and I stare at him.

"Mom died," he whisper-talks.

"Eh?" But I know what he just said. I look up at the ceiling. Maybe her and Chester are up there watching us after what they said at camp about heaven. But I can't believe his mom isn't still up at his place. Is it true? Mom'll be so mad I found out before her. Maybe Mrs. O'Brien is telling her right now.

He just looks at me. I think of what Mrs. O'Brien told Mom about the poison and Nurse Smiley, but it's too late to say anything even if it was true.

173

"She's in heaven now," I say, but I don't think so. It doesn't feel like she's anywhere. Don't even think heaven is where they say it is. "Streets are paved with gold there," I say. We sit for a long time. "You got *Jaysus* in your heart?"

"I don't know."

"You should if you want to go to heaven."

"Maybe I don't believe in God."

"But you have to or you won't go to heaven."

"Isn't the Landing good enough?"

"But you read her the Bible. You even said so." Now's my only chance so I take out my stuff and my Laura Secords.

"What's that?"

"Stuff I have to give you."

"Why?"

"I'll tell you later." I see his red jackknife on the floor by the bunks. "You got that Bible you read to your mom?"

"What do you mean?"

"Just want to show you something."

"I got it here."

"Can you find this?" I give him the paper Joycee gave to me. I still don't have a Bible and I don't care.

Tom opens his mom's Bible careful like he's peeling skin off an onion. Keeps looking at the paper matching up the words and numbers.

"Put it there. Sit here."

"Why?"

174

"I want to show you what blood brothers do. I know all about it. Now sit." We sit face to face, cross legs—Injun style—on the floor.

He won't look me in the eye.

I hold out my closed hands to him.

"First one brother would give the other a gift, like this. Pick a fist."

Tom touches my right hand. I turn them both and open them 'cause something's in each one anyway.

"These would be for you—if you were going to be my blood brother. Take them."

Tom looks into my hand and takes the broken china from old man Fitzroy's cabin. He takes the blue jay feathers I brought, and the carved 'geniality thing too, from camp, and puts them on the floor. He matches the two birds kissing, twists the feathers in his fingers, dangles the string of the carved thing in his hands like he's trying to make a cat's cradle with one hand.

"Get your knife," I say.

Tom turns and gets his knife. I know he'll like this because he likes his knife.

"This is the most important part of what blood brothers do. You can't be chicken."

"I'm not chicken," says Tom.

"Then cut my finger."

Tom takes my finger.

"Squeeze it real hard."

"I thought you weren't chicken," he says. Then he jabs me a good one.

"I just don't want to squirt any blood—ouch."

"There."

There was blood but no real hurt. More like surprise. "Now I'll do you."

"No I'll do it."

"Okay." If I can't cut him I don't know how I'll ever kiss him. Wish Mac Osler hadn't said about the kissing. "Now we have to put our fingers in each other's mouths." Maybe Thierry La Fronde did it when Margaret wasn't watching, but I made it up. "Close your eyes." I taste wet on my lips and wet lips on my finger as Tom takes my blood. I tighten my lips on his finger a bit before he pulls it away, so I know I kissed part of him, at least. I keep my eyes closed for a sec. "Now read that thing from the Bible."

Tom's finger runs down the middle of the page, leaving a mark, and then stops. He checks the paper I gave and then looks again at the page. He rasps his throat: "Behold how good and how pleasant it is for brethren to dwell together in unity."

Damn Joycee. "What's brethren?" I ask, like no one could ever know the answer.

But Tom does. "It means brother. I know that. Mom told me that. She said Ojibway are my brethren."

"Oh."

"We have to eat these." I peel the tissue off the Laura Secords. "Strawberry crème for you. Maple walnut for me."

176

I jump because his father squeaks open the door and stands there.

"Come for a swim."

I figure he's going to tell me to get the heck away from Tom or something. Like the time when we were little and Tom and me always walked around everywhere in the summer with arms around each other's shoulders. "Boys don't do that," his dad had said. So we held hands. "You look like a couple of queers for God sakes." Said that, too. So after that we didn't touch so much. Even Mom said old queers like to touch kids. Give them candy and money. But I don't think Tom cares.

Tom slips his bottoms off to be bare naked. I do the same. No questions about that. We run naked out onto the steps and down the hill, our dinks flipping and flapping with each step and hop. It's good to run naked and know we aren't really being bad 'cause there's a grown-up there doesn't mind. Mrs. O'Brien sure can't see us from here.

Bet Tom's surprised I don't care. And he's kind of happy then, not serious as usual, and he runs to the end of the dock and I follow him, cannonball into the water. I hate thinking it's the end of August, with the water like warm soup and weeds up from the bottom. But I'm not afraid. We tread water and I watch his dad drop his towel to the dock, looking like the mighty Hercules and he raises his big policeman arms and dives headlong into the water. He's under for a long time until his sputter and splash when he comes to the surface out past the raft.

Tom laughs and splashes me, and heads out to the raft. I follow him over the weeds and at the raft we climb onto the prickly carpet. It gives my bum goosebumps. Tom dives and I jump back into the water and head for shore. It always feels good to be bare-skin naked. And each wave and splash we make this morning has its own lighted edge from the sun.

I hear Tom call behind me and blow bubbles in the tune of that song about strangers in the night. I laugh but then he's close by and then I feel his hand on my leg, which is so good to know his touch. But the tickle goes right up my leg to where I know it's wrong without him even touching it. The kids at camp called me a fairy. They didn't have to say fairies were bad. You could tell in the way they said it. And I can't breathe. I shake my foot free and head for shore. I don't know if a person your own age touches you is that bad? I don't want people calling me a fairy-homo-queer like they know something I don't.

"I have to go!" I shout. No sounds come from the water, just splashing. I guess he doesn't care I'm leaving. He doesn't say anything. I'm stumbling up the rocky bank, have to reach out in front until I'm off the rocks.

And later in the afternoon the wind is blowing strong and a real chill comes down from the north. The cedars are fighting against the wind and the river is full of whitecaps. O'Briens' flagpole clinks when the rope flaps against it. Will we ever get back to the Sargasso?

There's us up on the movie screen, at the fair. Margaret with white gloves and party shoes and me looking like her sister, and we're stuffed in with other kids, into fake boats that sit in a trough, not real water. I always hoped the water was connected to the river and you could escape in your own little boat. We go round and round, keep smiling at the camera.

SEVENTEEN

"Your father has a job for you."

Never figured out why it's always "your father" and "your mother" and not his wife or her husband.

"What's he want?" says I, thinking it's like, *Go get some water,* or *Pull up the boats.*

"It's at the fair, in town."

"Oh yeah?"

I never had a job before except helping the little ones with swimming lessons, but now even swimming's over. This is going to be a real job. Joycee won't have her real job till next year. "Do I get to make money?"

"It's a job, don't be smart," says Dad.

"What kinda job?"

"You'll find out when you get there," he snaps. And he's in a mood like I never seen. I don't say anything but I know I haven't been home long enough to do something wrong unless I did before I went to camp and can't remember now—like leaving an experiment or some food under something like an old rotten Easter egg or that.

He used to drop me and Margaret there for the day once I was old enough for us to go on our own. Before we left, Mom would say I have to keep an eye on Margaret. Don't let any dirty old queers give her or me money or candy. They just do that so they can touch you. I never understand that. Everybody touches everybody. It's just not bad. Anyways, now I'm going to be on my own. No more watching Margaret. Now I'll have a new boss. Maybe I'll be calling numbers in the bingo tent or making cotton candy or maybe in Cattle Castle with all the farm animals.

"I can't wait," I say to Margaret.

"Are you going to tell Tom?" she says.

"No, he'll be jealous." Once he worked at the fair shucking corn for a week. "He knows what it's like to have a job."

"You don't need to go there anymore," says Mom, "after what he and his mother put us through this summer."

"His mom died."

"Mrs. O'Brien told me and that's just too bad, but we'll just have to leave well enough alone."

Now I'm thinking again it's what we did in the water why I have to have a job. I want to pray more not to be a fairy but all's I can think about is that now we're blood brothers and he's my duty. It's something that will grow now.

When we get into town the next morning, Dad drops me at the fairgrounds and says he'll get me in a couple hours. I go where I see the most people, but they all look busy. I don't want to ask anyone anything. It doesn't look like a fair, just canvas tents, but already the grass is tromped where people and tractors have been.

There's this big trailer house and tattooed men in blue jeans standing around, smoking, not shaved either, and women too with fags hanging out of the corners of their mouths. Some of them ignore me and some give me a nod and a grin. This fat lady, all dimples in her elbows, takes me to where I'm going to work. Already there's loud organ music all around.

We walk by guys putting together the Ferris wheel and the new Tilt-A-Whirl. Their shirts are off and they're sweating with the work. They're all deep browned like perfect marshmallows—not the one I smacked on Joycee's arm. One's back is black with a tattoo of an eagle. Hands greasy. All of these guys veiny and hard, as if every muscle has a reason to be there. We keep walking and the big lady takes me right up to my ride, the Scrambler, across from the House of Horrors and there's this thing the size of a phone booth where I guess we always bought our tickets.

"Dis where you wort," she says. She sounds funny like maybe she's a real Injun, a *squaw* like I heard Mom call Tomahawk's mom. "Your shif eight to five."

All's I can see, behind the plastic window, is a board to sit and a little shelf to put tickets on. She lets me climb on the board to see what it's like. My feet don't touch the ground which is good because the floor is all sticky-looking, probably from spilled pops. Everything inside smells like old french fries, outside smells like frying donuts and corn dogs. "Come bat tomorrow. Don't be late," she says.

I walk around the fairgrounds and watch the big guys build more of the other stuff and then I wait for Dad outside the gate by the ditch, pinching the last purple ends of the loosestrife and batting the cattails. Big guys walk by in groups to finish up the rides. They're smoking now. I recognize some from earlier. There are more tattoos on the tops of their arms except some have them below their elbows. Their hands are big from using them. No one looks at me.

Soon there's no one around. I wait some more. My stomach growls. Towards the valley the sky is the colour of peaches and a clear blue you don't get in the day, and then the colours are gone. Lights flash bright behind the fence—first it's just the parking lights and then the ride lights start to flicker. Soon all the rides are spinning and twirling and there's even music but no people. It all looks like a big toy. No people in the way, no people to wreck it. Then the guys walk by but this time swigging beer out of bottles and belching and shouting and whooping, or punching and headlocking.

"Hey kid, want to come to town?" says one guy and they all laugh. "Poor kid bin there all afternoon," I hear the guy say. There's a car horn honking and honking while I'm watching them walk along the road towards town. Dad waves at me for a few seconds before I figure out it's him. He's a lot happier and I wonder what he did to make him like that, especially taking so long.

"Hungry?" he says.

My head's starting to hurt along with my stomach. "Yep," I say.

"Burgers at the Wayward Bus?"

"Sure."

At home I throw up.

"You shouldn't be eating that fair food. I knew a woman and it killed her on her wedding day doing that," says Mom. "Literally burned a hole through her stomach. They had to turn right around and bury her the very same day. Can you imagine being buried in your wedding dress?" she squeals, then adds, "Just as well I suppose." I don't say anything else about the burger.

I can't sleep, 'cause tomorrow there'll be all the rides and games going and everyone from the Landing and even people from school's going to see me with my job. So Dad drives me to the fair and this time things are different. There's colours and music and people in striped outfits sitting in little striped booths that look like candy canes. All smiling and clean. I didn't see any of them yesterday. I say I'm working there and they tell me to come in from the side from now on. Mostly everyone is smiling now and all looking fresh and no more setting up. It's all ready. All waiting for folks to come and have fun. All the canvas-covered tents are open and guys are yelling

184

to throw balls. Women are talking into megaphones to come play bingo. I have to walk quick now to get to the trailer, since customers are starting to wander around.

They give me money called a float, that adds up to about forty dollars exactly and it's all in ones and twos and a couple of fives and some rolls of coins and a box I have to keep it in.

"Do I get a uniform?"

"A what?"

"People at the gate got uniforms."

"People at the gate don't work for us. Get going kid." Now there's a flood of kids and grown-ups all walking to the rides and games, so I run and the box is clanging.

"Sompin's wrong with it, kid," says this smiling guy. "Don't sell any tickets for now. You the kid from yesterday? Someone finally pick you up?"

"Yep."

It's the same guy who talked to me yesterday, thick arms and a heart tattoo just above his left hand and a snake near the muscley part of his other arm. Long blonde hair, too, kinda stringy like he needs a shampoo or a comb.

There's another guy squatted down under it with wrenches and tools so I have to sit in the booth anyway. "Ride's broken," I say to strangers as if I know all about it. I watch the guy squirm under it, his arms blue with tattoos and veins thick as telephone cords under the skin. Cigarette pack squeezed in his t-shirt sleeve. I look at my arm and it's some skin and nothing about veins. Where'd they come from? Even the dads at Baird's

185

Landing and Tomahawk's dad never had something like this. And all these guys got blue jeans, maybe stiff with dirt, like Mom says, and they smoke and say *fuck* this and *fuck* that. They all got cowboy boots, too.

And the muscley guy squirming under the ride's out now and on his feet and a lot shorter than the long-haired guy. He's missing two front teeth and all his *s*'s sound like *f*'s. "There, Joe. Your fuckin' ridef up and fuckin' ready for the little baftardf." He smiles anyway. Winks at me. Makes a spitting sound when he laughs at what he said.

The ride gets going and the little guy goes away but the guy from yesterday stays. Shouts at me: "Name's Joe." He's friendly looking with wrinkles round his eyes and arms like Popeye or Bluto. "You can sell tickets now."

"Name's Doug," I shout back.

I'm glad I got my jeans, too. No cowboy boots, only runners, 'cause yesterday I dressed nice for the job—Mom's idea, like back-to-school clothes from last year, the make-you-stiff kind that you can't get dirty.

I sit on my high bench like a bird on a perch, little metal screen for me to peek through or more like for people to look at me on display. Mostly kids come and they can hardly see over the counter. All my tickets and change are on it and one kid shoves the counter as hard as he can and it tips and all the money clangs to the floor where it's sticky and I can't get it, not now.

The fat Injun lady from yesterday comes along with her little kid and tells me to take a break and come back in fifteen minutes. All she does all day is goin' around to be other people's breaks. I get off the perch and dig the money out of the guck on the floor. Her little Injun kid sits on the bottom of the booth where I spilled my money and plays there while the big fat mom sits over him and I think if the perch snaps she'll squash him.

I take off to Cattle Castle to see if there are any puppies or pigs. Mom made me PB and J, better than for school when we have to make our own. And in Cattle Castle there was something going on, but now it's all finished and the people gone. Sandwich is squashed and I lick the paper. Glad I'm outta that camp. I wish Tom was here, too, but I can't see him if he's thinking of that touching stuff. It'll make us dirty old men, make us go to hell.

Fifteen minutes not enough to eat squashed PB and J, and the Injun lady looks sour when I get back. She doesn't say anything, just goes. At the end of the afternoon I go back to the trailer with my money and tickets and this wrinkly, white-haired lady behind jail bars counts it. "You owe me twenty-three dollars," she says, and her voice is deep down, like a man's.

"I don't got twenty-three dollars."

"We'll take it out of your twenty-four you made today. Here's a dollar." And she licks her thumb and snaps a buck from my bills and tosses it at me. "Keep an eye on your cash, kiddo," and then she hacks some gravel in her throat.

So for all that day I made a dollar and I wonder if there's still money stuck on the floor.

"How'd it go?" says Mom, sounding the same as when she talks to Dad, head down to the sink, washing something, not paying attention.

"Good."

"Are you rich?" says Dad.

"Know better when I get paid."

"Didja get to go on the rides?" says Margaret.

"Whenever I want."

My eyes won't stay open even for the comics, but still I'm thinking I can't wait till the other kids come and see me work at a real job.

But another two days and I'm still short of cash and only have a dollar to show for it. "I can't go to work," I say.

"You sick?"

"Yeah."

"Work will make an honest man of you," says Dad.

"No one'll talk to me."

"That's not what you're there for," says Dad. "You'll disgrace your father. I got you that job."

I can't tell them about the money, and what I said about no one talking to me isn't true because Joe talks to me even when his buds come by. He probably thinks I'm a girl in that cage. When I'm not selling tickets I watch Joe's arms up to the rolled-up sleeve, plopping kids into the seats. He squeezes them tight each time, like they're breakable or something, then he bangs the gate shut. I think it would feel good to have him plunk me into the ride. How can a body grow that big? Before my break that day I count all my money.

"I'm only leaving twenty dollars," I tell the fat lady before my break. Can someone tell I'm carrying lots of money and then pickpocket me? "Show me my twenty," I say when I get back. She scowls and grabs her kid and yanks his arm hard enough that he squeals and then they go.

Now I know I'll make money. I'll probably get at least twenty a day, which is more than I ever made before.

I look out my cage and it's a surprise to see Tomahawk and the Smiley brats walk by my ride but they won't come to the window, they just stand there and Tom counts out his money. I want to call him but he's too far away, so they go. Other years Tom made me go on rides I didn't want to go on and we had a good time. We did the Glass House and I remember seeing the Wall of Death on Harleys. And those times it was us, our arms around each other's shoulders.

"You in there?" I hear, and Margaret peers over the ledge, white-gloved hands over her eyes. And it's Mrs. O'Brien I see next, dressed like she's going to church, all gloves and even a hat on her bun. I'm surprised because I see Mom looking proper, too, with makeup and her pearls. She never came

189

before, Dad always brought us. Joycee's there, even though she's not allowed to go to movie matinees.

"You wearing your party shoes?"

"Mister, how much is a ticket?" Margaret says pretending she didn't hear me.

"Why's Mom here?" I say.

"She yelled at Dad on the phone and cried."

"Oh."

"Joycee's dad brought us all. He's on his summer vacation. He says he doesn't care if it's not God's will, he wants to have some fun."

Joycee won't come over to the window.

"Tell Joycee I saw Tom earlier," I say.

"These your folks?" says Joe.

"Yeah."

"Do they want a ride?"

"Okay."

And Margaret's eyes go real big and Joe grabs her around her waist and plops her in the ride like she's a marshmallow, and then Joycee, too. They scream and Joycee even smiles, doesn't know I can see her. It's fun to watch people when they don't know you're watching them. Seem more innocent, like you could like them a whole lot more. Then the ride stops and they have to go, because it's not my break yet.

At lunch I keep a lookout for them or Tom but I guess they're having their own fun so I go to see the Real Amazon Woman and she's dead and looks like dried-out paper mashay.

I hurry over to see the rubber boy, and he's better because he's really alive—he sits there in big diapers and has these baby legs and flicks them back and forth like there's no bones. I figure that's not fake and then it's time to go back. After I get back, Tom's at my window all of a sudden like there were all these kids before and then he's there. "When you finished?"

"Four."

He stands there and I know he's not going to hang around until then.

"Joycee's here."

"I already saw her."

"See rubber boy?" I say.

"Nope."

My heart beats and makes my hands shake, too. "Better'n Amazon Woman—least he's alive, you know. Remember the Harleys? Hey, maybe we can go for a swim when I get home."

"Got any money?"

When he says this I can't talk but I nod. It's my duty now. We're blood brothers and that's your job. I hope he knows. But what if that's the only reason he came up to the window?

"Here's ten," I say and even so it's not very much 'cause by now I saved exactly twenty-seven. I should have given him half but he's got the Smiley brats with him. "Brother," I say, then I ask, "you going to see your friends?"

"Who?"

"Them guys you hang out with? Or Jerry Mapother?"

191

"Which ones?"

"The Landing guys."

"Haven't seen them since you shot the blue jay. They took off. They don't like swimming, or even having showers, I bet. They stink."

I want to tell him they were the ones who said only homos take showers but it doesn't matter. What they say is probably as stupid as what anyone says.

"Anyway Dad says we're moving up to the Landing year-round," says Tom.

"To the Landing?"

"He just never wanted to leave Mom alone out there in the winter. Now he says I can go to school and he can work and he can pick me up and drop me off at school. Doesn't have to worry about her alone now she's gone."

"So we'll be neighbours?"

For the first time I can remember, Tom looks me right in the eyes, doesn't look away. Like he's giving me something he doesn't give anyone else—not Jerry or Joycee or the other kids at all. He doesn't look down. And I feel like it's the first time I ever saw him, first time he ever saw me. Like we know now we're blood brothers. And if he had to, he'd pay me back.

He goes away from the window, not a *Thanks pal*, or nothing, just goes, but I'm rich enough anyway.

"You're not buying cowboy boots," says Mom.

"It's *my* money."

"Your father didn't go to all that trouble so you could waste your money on cowboy boots."

"It's not fair."

Before we close that night, Joe gives me a fag through the window and leans against the booth. He holds my hand steady with his rough hands—same hands he plunks those kids in the seats— lights it for me, and I'm there coughing but not like in the woods when I have to smoke them quick. Nope. I sit there. Him talking about the pack-up, mostly to himself.

"You from these parts?" says Joe, his wrinkly eyes smile at me.

"Yeah," I say, my eyes stinging from the smoke. "An' you?"

"Not too far. Cleveland, anyway."

"That's far. I think my mom's cousints live around there."

He shouts to one of the other guys from the other ride and then says to me, "See you tomorrow kid," and walks off. I wonder if he ever made blood brothers.

I finish my fag because no one can see me in the booth. Maybe God thinks smoking is bad but at least he's the only one who knows. I think of all the stuff me and Tom can do together at the Landing, every weekend this coming year. Leaf forts, snow forts, bobsledding, too. His place won't be empty in the winter anymore.

Next day after my break, there's a crowd of people and the ride not going. I look through all the bodies until I see Joe on the ground and everyone crowded around. His mouth open, no smiling wrinkles. Soon men in white come and lift him onto a bed on wheels and take him away. A scrawny old guy, who takes over for Joe, doesn't say a word. It's hot and the busiest day so far. My pants are soaked from sweat and I can't wait to go home.

"Here's your dough," says the deep-voice lady and she hands me two ones.

"But…"

"Don't need you anymore kiddo."

"Is it Joe?"

"What?"

"Is the ride finished?"

"For you it is. You're fired. Don't need crooks here. Beat it kiddo."

"But…"

"Count your blessings kiddo. Get out while you can." And I know the big lady and the little kid didn't like me being careful. If Joe wasn't hurt, he'd have stood up for me.

I walk to the gate and wonder what it'll look like tomorrow and after that. Soon Joe and his pals will take apart the ride and then take it somewhere else. I didn't even get to go on any rides.

"They said they didn't need me."

"What?" and my dad is in his after-town good mood, so he's not listening anyway. He's just smiling at the road in front of us.

"Said I stole, but I know who did."

Dad just drives.

That night I dream about school, look out the window, see the fair in the yard. Someone selling tickets in that sticky booth. Someday I'll have cowboy boots for sure and Tom will, too. We'll be the guys fixing stuff. When he gets better, Joe'll show us how.

EIGHTEEN

Never many winter shots with the movie camera, only pictures of us coming down the driveway or standing on a snow fort or making angels in the snow. Barely moving. Like she was watching us without us knowing, instead of the other way around. But someone drops the camera or maybe Mom is trying to wind it while it's still going and you can see the treetops blowing in the breeze like they were when it was spring and then both sides were showing two shades of green against the blue sky, and then nothing.

The morning is hot and summer is back. Heat's going to give us an Injun summer. Maples out on the island are already turning yellow and red.

Mom starts to talk even before we're out of our beds. I can't get my eyes open to the bright and Margaret is picking the sand out of hers.

"We're moving to the city," I hear.

"For how long?" says Margaret. I think maybe I'm finishing dreaming.

"For good," says Mom.

"We can't," says Margaret and starts to cry.

"Your father and I have decided."

But I can't even swallow. Something huge stuck in my throat. My face burns. My lips close tight.

"Why?"

Mom doesn't say anything, just stands there.

"The stealing?" I ask.

"What stealing?"

"This is home," says Margaret.

"Mine too," I say.

I can only think it's not even the town we're moving to, it's the city. I know school kids in the town. Somehow I'd be able to see Tom if we moved to town, but not in the city.

"Your father... is going to live in the city, too."

"What do you mean?"

"He... won't be living with us."

Then I know for sure it's not my fault but maybe, like Margaret says, he likes Miss Harris or maybe 'cause Mom finally hated Baird's Landing too much. Or both.

There's no photo books on her table now or pieces of film to be glued.

"I bet it's Miss Harris," whispers Margaret. She doesn't even cry. We pick at our eyes and stare down at the sheets. Mom walks away.

"It's a good thing you're not working at that fair," she calls back. "One of the rides killed a man. It was bound to happen sooner or later."

"Who'd it kill?" I say.

"It's all there in your father's paper."

I never read his paper except for the funnies. But the headlines say: FAIR WORKER KILLED. In all the words I spot the name "Joe" and don't read the rest, just tear it out.

Joe dead. Big arms. Tattoos. Cigarettes. Hair. Friendly wrinkles. Thick greasy fingers giving me a cigarette through the little ticket cage. Rough hands holding my hand to light it. Only time I touched him. He touched me. All of that, dead. Like being touched by Tom. His soft foot on mine. Me holding Boston Justin while we slept. Chester's dad holding him, shaking. Dad's hand on my shoulder. Me in his arms, crying in his chest. Always a touch to look forward to.

Too much in my head now. Dad won't live with us, and maybe he doesn't like us or thinks we hate Baird's Landing as much as Mom does. Margaret doesn't cry at all. Maybe it's a mistake. No one says anything. It's a logjam in some river that can't hold it. Not like our wide, slow river.

I think about going over to Tom's, but I won't be able to no more. Never again. I wasted all that time not going over when I could have—when I was mad at him or wanted to see if he would come over to see me. No chance of ever going with him to the Sargasso Sea ever again. My whole face turns into a frown and my lips knot and I can't keep my face still as tears come out of me even more than when Dad took the nail out of my knee, more tears than I ever thought I had and I have to blow my nose or it feels like I really will drown. I hurry into my bedroom.

"*Maudite Chreest*! I'm not switching fucking schools," I yell over the wall. Mom stomps in, slaps me hard on the face and then holds my cheeks and looks at me and starts to cry and hold me real close to her bosoms like she hasn't for a long time, and so I put my arms round as much of her as I can and start to cry again. Then Margaret comes and starts to cry, too.

"I'm sorry," she says.

I say I'm sorry, too, sorry for ever thinking she's mean like Tomahawk says. She can't help it. At least she's still alive, like his mom isn't. At least I still got a mom and dad.

Can't think what'll happen if we aren't there to watch the river freeze or know when it's thawed up again. And who's supposed to watch O'Briens' and tell Dad to shovel the snow off the roof? Go get water?

"Can I still go to the same school?"

Mom nods but with that look where she sees something far away and nothing else. She doesn't mean it.

199

I know now I won't be the one at the Landing that lives there year-round anymore and Tom will take over with his Injun ways. But then no one else has parents getting split up like mine, which is almost like having someone die on you. Maybe relatives will feel sorry for me and treat me like I'm practically famous. Friends don't say anything about it to you, so maybe I'll get some of that. It's called divorce. Everyone will whisper that. Especially Mrs. O'Brien.

Maybe if we keep the house for coming up in the summers like other folks then I won't have to go to camp is all I can think now. And then I can see Tom. He's my brother now, and still will be.

I lie in my bed on the veranda, listen to Margaret breathe, wonder when our last night at the Landing will be. I think about that day on the Sargasso Sea, how Tom and me just sat there in the boat on the weeds while the river kept going past us. I wish I had pictures of that, like Mom does, pictures of being together and of everything being perfect on the calm water on top of the weeds.

I think of what Chester did, being sad or scared enough to kill himself. If I hadn't made Tom my blood brother I could do that now. I wouldn't feel the sadness anymore. But it's the blood keeping me here now. Hoping I'll be with him again. I wish we could have stayed stuck in the Sargasso Sea like those real sailors did, the ones who went crazy. Tom and me could have gone crazy together.

Maybe if we never left there, time wouldn't have passed, and they wouldn't have missed me, no storms would have happened, and I would never have had to go to camp. No one to say fairy, fairy, Frenchie. No one to make me scared of wanting his touch. His foot on mine.

ACKNOWLEDGEMENTS

Thanks to the caring guidance from Nightwood Editions, especially Silas White for his considerate editing and Michelle Winegar for her evocative design. Thanks to the support of the UBC Creative Writing Program, my colleagues, instructors, professors and especially Keith Maillard for his kind mentorship, and Maureen Medved for her unwavering faith in me. Thanks to the encouragement and support of the Banff Writing With Style gang. Thanks to everyone I ever enlisted to critique my work. Thanks to those who have ruminated, questioned and challenged. Thanks to my caring mother and father, whose appreciation of the arts has been a source of inspiration, and thanks to my family, brother, sisters, in-laws, nephews and nieces as well as dear friends, for their love and support. Thanks especially to my partner Bernard who challenges me to do my best, bolsters me when I need it, and is here throughout.

ANDREW BINKS was a finalist in the Writers' Union of Canada Short Prose Contest and *This Magazine*'s Great Canadian Literary Hunt. His fiction, non-fiction, and poetry have appeared in *Galleon*, *Prism International*, *Harrington Gay Men's Literary Quarterly*, *Bent Magazine* and the *Globe and Mail*. After fifteen years in Vancouver, he has returned to Ontario. *The Summer Between* is Binks' first novel.